"Keep your distance!"

"You need not imagine that your identity gives you any rights concerning me."

Despite himself, Hal felt his temper rising. "What do you take me for? I have no intention of—"

"I am glad you chose to bring up the subject of your intentions, sir, because I am excessively interested to know what they might be."

Hal tried for a calmer note. "Annabel—"

"Mrs. Lett to you, sir."

"Oh, the devil!" he snapped, exasperated. "I am supposed to be your husband."

"Not by any will of mine."

The Captain's Return

Elizabeth Bailey

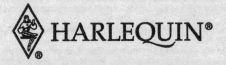

TORONTO • NEW YORK • LONDON
AMSTERDAM • PARIS • SYDNEY • HAMBURG
STOCKHOLM • ATHENS • TOKYO • MILAN • MADRID
PRAGUE • WARSAW • BUDAPEST • AUCKLAND

ISBN 0-373-30420-X

THE CAPTAIN'S RETURN

First North American Publication 2003

Copyright © 2002 by Elizabeth Bailey

Visit us at www.eHarlequin.com

Printed in U.S.A.

ELIZABETH BAILEY

grew up in Malawi, then worked as an actress in British theater. Her interest in writing grew and soon overtook acting. Instead, she taught drama, developing a third career as a playwright and director. She finds this a fulfilling combination, for each activity fuels the others, firing an incurably romantic imagination. Elizabeth lives in Sussex.

THE STEEPWOOD SCANDAL:

Chapter One

July 1812

It was what he had anticipated. But the confirmation did not make the news any more acceptable to Captain Henry Colton. There had been little hope of finding Annabel's circumstances to be otherwise. But to hear her spoken of as *Mrs Lett*!

The Captain took a hasty turn about the bare room. It seemed large in its barren state, empty of all furnishings. But Hal Colton's six-foot frame dwarfed the place.

Even in civilian clothes he was impressive, the green frock-coat of plain cut moulding across broad shoulders, and the muscle in his thigh evident under the buckskin breeches. His cravat was simply tied, and his boots decently polished. An air of command belied his six-and-twenty years, and from his bearing no one could mistake his calling, even without the dashing military moustache. Like his hair it was red-gold, in keeping, so his elder brother Edward maintained, with his temper.

He came to a halt in front of his informant. "You're sure of this, Weem? She is indeed married?"

His batman, a stunted individual upon whose enterprise and cunning Hal had relied heavily in the past, nodded vigorously. But there was a glint of mischief in his sharp eyes, and the Captain's blood quickened.

"What is it? Tell me at once, lunkhead, or I'll have your guts for garters!"

Weem grinned cheekily, arms akimbo over the rough serge coat he had donned by way of disguise, together with a slouch hat now crushed in one hand.

"Lunkhead, is it? And me an intelligence agent of the highest order!"

Captain Colton started threateningly across the room, and his batman threw up a hand in surrender.

"Keep yer hair on, guv'nor. I mean to tell you it all, yer know that."

"Then cut line! I'm in no mood for your funning."

From the window opposite, the Captain's brother broke in. "Have patience, Hal. After all, you've waited three years and more. A couple of minutes can't make much difference."

It made a deal of difference to Hal. And it had been by no wish of his that the intervening years had furnished no news of Annabel Howes. Ever since that appalling night, when their last hideous quarrel had culminated in his losing all claim to call himself a gentleman, the Captain had spared no pains to try to make all right. Despite being recalled to Spain, and leaving with his regiment the very next morning.

Annabel had resisted his every attempt to contact her. His letters had been returned unopened. Twice he had spent his hard-earned leave of absence in fruitless searching. Twice he had been turned away by old Benjamin Howes—first in London, and again at the family estates. No surprise there. Howes had been against him almost from the start, causing Annabel to break off their engagement.

Then had come this windfall, an estate bequeathed to him by his godfather. It was a modest place, but with a decent enough income derived from rents to encourage Captain Colton to sell out. He and his brother had driven across to look it over, travelling in the old-fashioned phaeton he had left at the family home during his long absence. It was, he averred, in good enough condition for general use.

"I'm not wasting my blunt on a new one yet a while."

But horses were another matter. He had brought his own and Weem's mounts back from the Peninsula, but a pair had to be purchased to go between the shafts of the phaeton. He had chosen to try their paces on this journey, rather than make it in his brother's flashy new curricle.

Weem had followed his master on horseback from the Colton estates some fifty miles distant. His batman had known full well how important was this news to him!

"Well, Weem?"

The batman glinted up at him engagingly. "It ain't so bad as you think, guv'nor. The lady was married, but seemingly she's a widow."

A huge weight rolled off Hal's chest. He gave Weem a light buffet. "Rascal! I ought to darken your daylights!"

"Then you wouldn't nowise hear the rest of it, guv'nor."

Edward Colton strolled over to his brother's side. In bearing, no two men could be more dissimilar. His frock-coat of mulberry was cut rather for comfort than for elegance. His boots were serviceable, his cravat neat, and he was as countrified as the Captain was military.

"What is the rest of it, Weem? You're being damned mysterious!"

The Captain turned his head, and the June sun, slanting in from the window, glinted off his bright curling locks. "It's his stock in trade, Ned. The fellow's a sly trickster and should have been locked up years ago. I don't know why I bear with him."

"'Acos I gets results, that's why, guv'nor. Does yer want to hear what I've got to say, or not?"

He neatly dodged a large avenging hand, and slid out of reach, cackling. But upon the Captain's promising signal vengeance presently, he desisted and gave forth his tale.

Hal listened with growing dismay as he heard that Annabel was living in a quiet style, in a rural backwater somewhere in Northamptonshire. The village, Steep Ride, was apparently tiny, and the cottage Annabel was inhabiting was one of only three houses of any size in the immediate neighbourhood.

''She lives in a cottage? What the devil was this fellow she married—a pauper?''

''It's by way of being on the large side for a cottage, guv'nor, judging by those o' the labouring men roundabouts. But the lady's place goes by the name of End Cottage.''

''Cottage!'' reiterated Hal disgustedly. ''In the back of beyond, too!''

''No such thing, guv'nor,'' protested the batman. ''Plenty o' what you might call society round about. Only this here Steep Ride is the smallest o' the villages. Though there's the big house, in an estate owned by a nob by the name o' Tenison. And o' course in the middle there's this Abbey what everyone talks of where that there markiss were murdered.''

''Murdered?'' A sudden, if irrational, fear for Annabel caught at Hal's chest.

''Happened only a week or two back. Not that no one round there is cryin' over him. A bad 'un he were, they say, be he never so much a markiss.''

''Lord, is he talking of Sywell?'' cut in Mr Colton.

''What do you mean, Ned?''

''What's the name you said, Weem? Steep something?''

"Steep Ride, sir."

"Then it must be the same. Steepwood Abbey was Sywell's seat. Lord, Hal, it's the most appalling scandal! The whole town was talking of it. Not that it's anything new. The fellow has been notorious for years."

Captain Colton frowned deeply. "I've never heard of him."

His brother waved this aside. "You've been more or less out of the country for the last seven years. I'm telling you, there's been the devil's own work in Steepwood. First Sywell's wife ran away. That was a few months back. Disappeared without trace, and had half the tabbies rumouring that he'd killed her. Then it was found there was gold missing. And now the fellow's been slashed to pieces in his own bedchamber!"

Hal breathed somewhat heavily. "And this is where Annabel is living! What in Hades was the fellow about to bring her to such a hole?"

"What fellow?"

"This fellow she married. Lett, or whatever his name is." The Captain paused, arrested by a sudden thought. "Wait a minute. Why does that name ring a bell?"

"Does it?"

"There's something about it." He pondered it

in his mind. Had he heard it before? Was it possible he had known Annabel's husband? "Who was Lett, Weem? Did you find out anything about him?"

"Seemingly he was of our cut, guv'nor."

"You mean he was a soldier?"

"Aye. Nor he ain't chose Steep Ride for his missus."

Edward Colton leaned back against the wall, where clung remnants of a brocaded paper, faded and peeling. "What in the world is he talking about, Hal? And if Lett was an army man, you might well have met him."

Hal shook his head, intent upon his batman. "What do you mean, he didn't choose Steep Ride?"

Weem shrugged. "Seemingly the lady and the babe come there after he was killed."

"Babe?"

A sudden dread premonition seized Captain Colton. He reached out an unsteady hand to grasp at his brother's shoulder, but his blue-grey eyes were fixed on his batman.

Weem was looking smug. "Ah. Wondered as how you'd take that bit of it, guv'nor. Nor you won't like it when I tells you that this here babe has a noddle o' red hair."

"Good God!"

Hal hardly heard Ned's comment. A heavy pulsing entered his chest and his brain felt as if it were going to explode. His throat tightened, and his voice seemed not to wish to obey him.

"How—how old? The babe. How old is it?"

Weem considered the question, trouble gathering in his sharp-featured face. "Just a toddler, guv'nor. I'd say not much more'n two—three at most."

"Oh, dear Lord," groaned Ned.

Captain Colton could not speak. What havoc had he wrought that fateful night? Had he not dreaded this very outcome, lying sleepless night after night in a crude cot in cantonments in Spain? Or bivouacking by an impromptu fire, supping on stewed rabbit, augmented by a potato or two filched from a nearby field? Weem had always been expert at ferreting for food to eke out the most meagre of rations. Would he had long ago had the sense to send him ferreting after this.

The nightmare of his worst fears realised! Yet when Annabel had so steadfastly refused to answer his letters, he had at length supposed that fortune had favoured them. But it had not been so. Had Annabel turned to him in the extremity of this unlucky accident? No, she had not. Hurt rose up, as sharp and bitter as when she had first rejected him.

"Well, that explains the locality," said his brother musingly, recovering from his first astonishment. "I wonder if it was Howes who set her up at Steep Ride."

"Who else?" said Hal bitingly. "Why the devil couldn't the old curmudgeon have come down off his high ropes? If he'd only sent me word—"

He broke off, becoming aware of his batman's steady regard. Useless to suppose that Weem had not already guessed the sum of it. But there was no need to bandy words in his presence that must necessarily wreck Annabel's reputation.

"You've done well, Weem. I'll want every last detail, mind, but that can wait."

Dismissed, the batman withdrew, leaving Hal confronting the accusing eyes of his senior. He threw up a hand.

"You need not look like that, Ned! I did everything I could to make it right. I promise you, I have a stack of letters to prove it."

"Returned unopened," agreed Mr Colton. "I know. You told me. What you didn't tell me—"

"I know. Devil take it, do you think I meant to do it?"

He crossed the parlour, as if he must avoid his brother's gaze, and went to stare out of the window upon the unkempt lawns. Only a short time ago he had been agreeing with Ned upon the number of gardeners required to return them to a semblance of order. His godfather had been old and ailing for some time, and the place had been allowed to deteriorate. How little he now cared!

"It was at a ball that it happened," he disclosed, without turning round. "We had not met since she broke off our betrothal. We quarrelled mightily. We were both too much empassioned to have any rationality left. Inevitable, I suppose. So much hot air." He turned suddenly, the blue-grey eyes afire. "And she did love me, Ned. I swear she still loved me!"

"Then, perhaps," agreed his brother meaningfully.

An obstruction lodged in Hal's chest. "You need not say it. What woman could continue to love the man who ruined her?"

Mr Colton came across the room. He was not near as tall, nor as broad in the chest as his brother, and his hair was less vibrant, tending more to gold. But he had the advantage of him in both years and temperament. Hal's tempestuous personality had ever been his undoing.

"You can't be absolutely sure, Hal, that she was ruined."

Hal's tone was bleak. "Can't I?"

"She is not precisely living in obscurity. Weem says there is some society there. Evidently she has acquired respectability."

"Respectability!"

"It's not lightly won, Hal. It is possible that Annabel did marry. Even if the child is yours, Annabel may have taken refuge under another's name."

"The devil she did!" Something clicked in the Captain's brain. He slammed a fist into his open hand. "*No*. Annabel didn't marry a man called Lett. There is no such man."

"How can you be sure?"

"I've remembered why it sounded familiar." Grimness settled in his chest. "Lett was the maiden name of Annabel's mother."

His brother was silent for a moment. But Hal's first shock was fading. Not for nothing was he a soldier. He was a captain, in command, given to swift decisions. What was needed now was not regret, but action. He stiffened his shoulders.

"What will you do?" asked Ned frowningly.

"Oh, I know what to do!"

His brother began to look alarmed. "Now, Hal—for the Lord's sake, think before you act!"

"I've thought for three years. I'm done with thinking."

"Oh, dear Lord! *Hal!*"

But Captain Colton was already on the move. Before he reached the door, his brother caught his arm. "Wait, Hal!"

He turned. Removing the hand that imprisoned him, he grasped it strongly. "Ned, I'm coming home with you, so you'll have every opportunity to argue. But let me advise you not to waste your breath. You can say what you like, but you won't change my mind."

Mr Colton grinned. "You always were a head-strong devil."

Hal's smile was twisted. "So I may be. But in this case, Ned, there's a matter of honour at stake. I have no choice."

The kitchen bench and two of the dining chairs had been brought out and set under the shade of a great chestnut. It was situated just upon the boundary, but it obligingly spread its branches to encompass a good part of Annabel Lett's garden. A circumstance that enabled her to receive her two visitors in a much pleasanter setting on a hot

Saturday in early July than was to be had in the tiny formal parlour within the cottage.

The visitors occupied the chairs, while Annabel took the bench. She was dressed in a sprigged gown of a soft green lawn that brought out the colour of her eyes, although its cut and style were far from fashionable. Its modest neckline, round and plain, and its three-quarter sleeves, together with the frilly cap that covered much of Annabel's dark hair, gave her an air of respectability.

It was a pose that Mrs Lett had cultivated with care and diligence. And if she had not entirely succeeded in subduing the restless spirit that lurked deep within—which now and then broke out, to her regret, in hasty words—she flattered herself that she had fooled most of her acquaintances in their reading of her character.

But the two ladies present were such particular friends that Annabel felt able to relax her strict guard. She would not have hesitated to entertain them in the larger family room, where Rebecca was permitted to run wild and all was generally at sixes and sevens. But this arrangement allowed little Becky to dash about the garden under her mother's eye, leaving Janet free to pursue her numerous chores.

Which was as well, for Annabel thought her

visitors would have burst with frustration if they had felt themselves obliged to hold their tongues in the presence of the maid. The subject under discussion was far too interesting. Especially since it concerned the man most people had settled upon as having done away with the dissolute Marquis of Sywell up at the Abbey.

"Can it be true, do you think?" asked Charlotte Filmer.

Jane Emerson, a slim brunette with little countenance except a pair of soft brown eyes, gave her characteristic gurgling laugh.

"I should think it all too likely, Mrs Filmer. Have we not all been puzzled as to why Solomon Burneck should have remained loyal to that wretched man? Nothing could more surely explain it than if he had indeed been Sywell's own son. Don't you think so, Annabel?"

"Yes, if only it had come out before the Marquis was murdered," agreed Annabel, accepting with a word of thanks the pebble pressed into her palm by her daughter, who ran off again to find another. "To put it about only when Burneck himself has fallen under suspicion seems to me in itself suspicious."

"Very true," agreed Charlotte, and a little

shudder ran through her. "I have always found him sinister."

Mrs Filmer was a gentle female, a great many years Annabel's senior, but they shared a common bond in the isolation of an existence without the support of a husband. Charlotte's daughter was grown up now, and had last season gone to London as companion to the Tenison chit—a piece of good fortune for which Mrs Filmer was still thanking Providence.

"Oh, I am perfectly happy to have Solomon for the villain," said Jane merrily. "Why, he looks a very devil, with that hooked nose, and his horrid black clothes. Thin lips are a sign of meanness, you know, and he has the horridest eyes of anyone I've ever met. Set so narrow and close."

Annabel could not help laughing as she placed the pebble among the growing pile beside her on the bench. "Jane, you are outrageous. What appalling prejudice! I pity your pupils, who are obliged to look to you for example."

"Fiddle! I am responsible only for their deportment and their performance in the dance. I have nothing to do with the formation of their *minds*.'

In fact, as Annabel knew, Miss Emerson was one of the more popular teachers at the Guarding

Academy in nearby Steep Abbot. Jane had a deceptively demure manner in social situations, but among friends—which term wholly encompassed her students—she exhibited a liveliness of mind, and an endearing warmth that made Annabel sorry for her circumstances. But Jane would have none of it.

"Don't waste your pity on me, Annabel, for I am perfectly content with my lot," she had said gaily. "I learned early to be so. I was ever a "plain Jane", and it is unlikely I should have caught myself a husband, even had it been possible for me to make a come-out."

Annabel might doubt this privately, but she had said no more on the subject, feeling the more thankful for their friendship that permitted Jane these small respites on her one free Saturday each month. Her company was a boon to Annabel, who could only admire the generosity of heart that left Jane with neither malice nor envy towards others, in particular the more flamboyant and adventurous of the Guarding teachers—like Desirée Nash, who had broken away earlier this year and ended by marrying Lord Buckworth.

"But don't you think, if Solomon Burneck had been Sywell's son," asked Mrs Filmer, bringing the conversation back to the point at issue, "that the Marquis would have got rid of him?"

"Oh, yes," agreed Jane, setting one graceful leg over the other so that the soft white muslin slithered, "if Sywell *knew*. You don't suppose he counted up his by-blows, do you, Mrs Filmer? They must be all over the countryside!"

"Jane, you shocking creature!" protested Annabel. "Pay no heed to her, Charlotte."

But Mrs Filmer was plainly amused, though she tutted in a fretful way, too. "She is right, of course. Oh, dear, how wretched it is that that dreadful man should be able to scandalize everyone even from beyond the grave!"

"What I want to know," said Jane more seriously, reaching absently for one of Becky's pebbles and playing it between her fingers, "is whether you had this from your usual source, Annabel. You get all the news before the rest of us only because Aggie Binns tells it to your Janet. It is too bad!"

Aggie Binns was a wizened diminutive creature who lived a short way from Annabel in a cottage near the village pump. Aggie had been taking in laundry for around thirty-five years, and was the main source of all the gossip emanating from the Abbey. This was because she had for years now been the only female willing to set foot in the place.

"It is not Janet. Janet would scorn to listen to Aggie's gossip. It comes to me through Young Nat's mother. You know she helps Aggie with the laundry."

Young Nat, who inhabited with his mother one of the little workman's cottages across the green, was by way of being Annabel's handyman, although he spent a part of each day working the smithy at Farmer Buller's place at Steep Abbot.

"Yes, but if Aggie had known a tidbit like this," pursued Jane, "she would not have kept it to herself for so long."

"Very true," agreed Charlotte. "The wretched woman does nothing but spread evil everywhere she goes, dragging that little laundry cart."

The conversation was suspended for a moment as the diminutive Miss Lett, coming up with another treasure, spied the theft perpetrated by Jane Emerson and set up a protest.

"Oh, I do beg your pardon, Becky," uttered the culprit contritely, holding out the errant pebble.

"Say thank you," reproved Annabel as her daughter snatched it away.

A pair of big blue eyes peeped defiantly up at

Miss Emerson under the red-gold mop of hair, which young Miss Lett invariably refused to allow to be confined under the mob cap suited to her years.

"I don't think Becky feels that I deserve to be thanked," commented Jane on a tiny laugh, "and I'm sure I don't blame her. It is a pretty pebble, Becky, and I am very sorry for taking it away without asking you."

Rebecca cast a doubtful glance up at her mother's face.

"There now," said Annabel. "Miss Jane didn't mean it, you see. Now say thank you politely."

Instead, Becky's gaze came back to "Miss Jane". With a sudden bright smile, she offered her the pebble to hold. It was accepted with becoming gratitude. Matters now being settled to everyone's satisfaction, little Miss Lett thought proper to return to her labours, leaving the ladies free to pursue their interrupted discussion.

Jane was vehement in her suspicions of Solomon Burneck. "If Aggie Binns had it from Solomon that he is Sywell's by-blow, it is certain that he intended for it to be repeated."

"Yes, but she didn't have it from Solomon," objected Annabel. "She got it from his cousin."

"What cousin? I didn't know he had a cousin."

"Had you not heard? Apparently this female cousin came to the Abbey in a panic, having heard that Solomon had fallen under suspicion of the Marquis's murder. It was she who let it out to Aggie."

"How foolish! Or doesn't she know what Aggie is like?"

"That's just what makes me think Solomon intended for it to be spread abroad," said Annabel.

Charlotte was instantly convinced. She nodded wisely under the frill of her cap that rippled with the movement. "Yes, I see what you mean, Annabel."

"No, I think we must vindicate Solomon," decided Jane, in an abrupt about-face, dropping Becky's pebble back among its fellows. "Unless his cousin has a reason to lie for him, it must be true. And one can scarce blame him for concealing it before this. I mean, if one had a father whose conduct was so excessively shocking, one would be at pains to hush it up. And Solomon Burneck has always condemned the Marquis. He has forever been quoting that piece from the Bible which instructs us that every dog must have his day. Yes, Solomon is certainly innocent."

Annabel could not help laughing. "You are readily convinced, Jane. I only hope you may not be made to look nohow by yet more dreadful revelations that prove him guilty beyond doubt.''

Before either of her visitors could answer this, a call from the kitchen interrupted them. A woman of dour aspect, tall but sturdy of figure and clad in the grey low-waisted gown of a servant, came hurrying towards the group under the tree.

''What is it, Janet?''

''It's the reverend from Abbot Giles, ma'am. He's got a gentleman with him.''

Annabel rose. ''Mr Hartwell? Here in Steep Ride? I wonder what he wants with me?''

The other two ladies were looking equally puzzled. Beyond one welcoming visit, when Annabel first came into the neighbourhood, she had usually seen the Reverend Mr Edward Hartwell only on Sundays. And that at his church in Abbot Giles, when she attended the service. Indeed, she had the intention of going there tomorrow. Otherwise, Mr Hartwell had called upon her only on the occasion of Rebecca's birthday, bringing a gift—a most kind attention—but she would not celebrate her third until November. Yet here he was.

''I had better go in to him. Is he in the parlour, Janet?''

"He said not to disturb yourself, for he's coming out."

And indeed, the vicar was to be seen coming around the corner of the house at that moment. He was a man in his forties, dark-clad as befit his calling, who walked with an energetic step and had usually a cheerful air about him. But as he approached, Annabel thought he was looking a trifle solemn, and a shaft of dismay shot through her.

It was evident that his demeanour had struck her guests just as oddly. Charlotte sounded fretful.

"What can have happened?"

"Lord, is someone dead?" muttered Jane.

Annabel's instant thought was of her daughter. But that was ridiculous. Becky had been with them throughout. Besides, she was still happily engaged in locating pebbles to add to the trove on the bench.

Then it must be Papa. Heaven forbid it was his untimely demise! They had been at outs, but she could not cease to love him. Only surely it would be Mr Maperton who came to break such news. The lawyer was in her father's employ. Or was it indeed Mr Maperton who had asked Mr Hartwell to break the news? Had not Janet said that the vicar had a gentleman with him? Only there was no gentleman in sight at this present.

These rapid thoughts had barely passed through her mind when the reverend gentleman was upon her, bowing to the other two ladies, and then fixing Annabel with a gaze of gentle austerity as he took hold of both her hands.

"I had hoped to find you alone, Mrs Lett."

Instantly, both Jane and Charlotte were up.

"Shall we—?"

"I am perfectly ready to—"

"No, no," said Mr Hartwell, turning briefly in their direction. "On second thoughts, it may be as well for her friends to be at hand in such a situation as this."

Annabel was silent, unable to think beyond the impending horror of what she was going to be told. The vicar's eyes came back to hers, and then passed on to Janet.

"Ah. Perhaps it would be sensible for your maid to remove the infant? Your attention, my dear, cannot be upon her well-being in this extremity."

"Extremity?" It was both sharp and low.

Mr Hartwell smiled his reassurance. "There is no cause for alarm, Mrs Lett. I am the bearer of tidings more shocking than distressing."

These words did nothing to allay Annabel's fears. She turned with that automatic action which drives one through emergencies.

"Janet, take Becky into the house."

She watched her maid walk across the grass and scoop up her daughter. Rebecca protested, and a slight delay was occasioned by her insistence on Janet's gathering up the carefully selected store of pebbles from the bench. When the maid had slipped them into the pocket of her apron, there was yet recalcitrance. But Janet murmured soothingly—of cake, Annabel suspected—at which her daughter's protests ceased abruptly and she allowed herself to be borne away.

"Sit down, Mrs Lett."

Annabel sat down, vaguely aware that her two friends did likewise. She stared up into the vicar's face, noting that his air of solemnity had been replaced with an edge of excitement.

"Pray tell me quickly," she uttered rapidly. "This suspense is more than I can endure."

He dropped back a pace, letting go her hands. "Mrs Lett, I have been requested to break to you a piece of news which may, in its production of joy, prove overwhelming."

Benumbed, Annabel repeated it. "Joy?"

"Dear me, this is harder than I thought for,"

said the reverend gentleman, his portentous air deserting him. "Nothing in my experience has prepared me for such a situation as this. I hope I may be forgiven if I mangle the task. Mrs Lett, my news is nothing short of miraculous. Your husband is alive."

Annabel hardly heard the murmured expressions of astonishment. Her voice was faint.

"I beg your pardon?"

"Your husband, Mrs Lett!"

Annabel stared at him, blank with incomprehension. What husband? She had never been married, for she was a fallen woman. Rebecca was the nameless product of an act of lunatic passion. What in the world could the man be talking of?

He seemed to read her thought. "I am speaking of Captain Lett."

"Captain Lett?" repeated Annabel stupidly. But there was no Captain Lett!

"You believed him dead," went on Mr Hartwell earnestly, and with growing eagerness. "But it appears that the report was false. He had been severely wounded, and taken prisoner. He was able to get a message to his regiment, and negotiations were begun which ultimately ended with his release."

"Oh, Annabel, how fortunate!" came from Charlotte. "I am so happy for you."

Annabel's eyes turned towards her. Had she gone mad? Of all people in this village, Charlotte surely knew that she was not who she said she was. They had never overtly spoken of it, but hints enough had been passed for Annabel to know that Mrs Filmer had guessed the true situation, which had made it abundantly clear that her own was just the same.

"It is indeed miraculous!" said Jane Emerson warmly, and Annabel saw that her soft brown eyes were misted.

Annabel's gaze returned to the parson's face. "I don't understand."

"No wonder!"

"It is as he feared," agreed Mr Hartwell worriedly. "It is just why the Captain requested my intervention. I wonder if perhaps I should—"

He had taken a few paces towards the corner of the cottage as he spoke, but he broke off. With a wide gesture indicating the way he had first come, he turned back to Annabel.

"But here he is—in person. Now perhaps you will believe what I am saying, Mrs Lett."

A gentleman came into sight. A tall, broad-shouldered gentleman, clad not in scarlet regimentals, as might have been expected, but in frock-coat and breeches. He carried his hat in his hand, and the sun fell upon his head of bright red-gold hair, which was matched by a clipped moustache.

Annabel sat rooted to the spot. She heard nothing of what was said around her, for shock deprived her of everything but recognition of the stark, bare fact.

This was no husband—and no Captain Lett. It was Captain Henry Colton, the father of her illegitimate child.

Chapter Two

For a few breathless moments, Hal's poise near deserted him. He had made a dreadful mistake! Was this whey-faced creature—this demure little matron, becapped and respectable—was *this* his fiery Annabel? She had never been a beauty, but she'd been spirited. She'd had a special magnetism that had haunted his dreams, along with those flashing green eyes.

Then he realised that they were staring at him in both shock and bewilderment. That there was a gauntness in her cheeks where there had once been bloom. But recognition surfaced just the same. This was Annabel.

Disappointment thrust at Hal, driving down the guilt, and he was conscious of a craven wish that he had not come. But his scheme—designed to thwart the inevitable defiance of the remembered Annabel—was fairly embarked, and he was as well trapped himself as he had thought to trap his quarry.

He became aware of the cleric at his elbow, the innocent Mr Hartwell, whom he had suborned into establishing his claim in a bid to make it impossible for Annabel to repudiate him.

"Mrs Lett is a good deal overcome, sir."

An understatement. She was clearly near swooning with shock. There were two females fussing to either side of her, the younger of whom was despatched by the other to fetch a glass of water. He had not intended Hartwell to make so public an exhibition of the affair.

"I feared that it would prove overwhelming," he responded, and noted with dismay that Annabel's silent figure flinched at the sound of his voice. She evidently knew him.

The vicar's expression was expectant. It flashed through Hal's mind that his assumed role demanded more of him. He hesitated. Should he go to her? Would a true husband at this juncture seize her in his arms? He could not bring himself to do it! Not to the female staring at him in so bemused a fashion. He did not even know what to say to her.

In truth he had not planned beyond the softened presentation by a local man of the cloth. But then it had not occurred to him that he would find so altered a creature in the woman he had loved and wronged. Nor that he would meet with anything other than a rebuff. Hence Mr Hartwell.

"If Jane will only hurry with that water," came worriedly from the older female, who was chafing one of Annabel's hands. "I fear she may faint away, Mr Hartwell!"

"I never faint."

Hal felt his guts go solid. Annabel's voice was a thread, but he would have known it anywhere. Its clear tone was in his head in too many recollected utterances to be mistaken. Deep inside the stranger he was confronting lurked the woman he had known.

He knew that it behoved him to consolidate the position he had adopted, but some quality in Annabel's dull green gaze—it had used to be anything but lacklustre!—made him pause.

His soldiering instincts came to his rescue. When baulked by the enemy, retreat and regroup. He set his shoulders and summoned a hearty air.

"Perfectly true. To my knowledge, she never has fainted." He turned to the vicar. "All the same, I believe it will be best if we withdraw for a space, my dear sir, and allow my wife a little time to recover.''

Annabel stared after his retreating back. Wife? His *wife?* She became aware of coolness against her lips.

''Drink, Annabel.''

She did so, bringing up a wavering hand to clasp the cool glass. There her fingers encountered Jane's, bringing her a little more alert.

''I think I can manage.''

''Very well, but I will remain close by.''

The glass came into her full possession and Annabel drank deeply. Her head began to clear. But an odd sensation, as if she were living in a dream, possessed her.

If she was not asleep, then Hal was here! Hal, whom she had last seen on that fatal night which had shattered her then known life, casting her adrift in this alien sea. Forced to hide her identity under a living lie, that a false cloak of respectability might be cast over the shadowed little creature that was her innocent daughter.

Hal, whom she had been unable to forget—unable to forgive!—reminded daily by the growing likeness in Rebecca's face and hair. How had he traced her here? Why had he done so? Foolish question! The answer was in Mr Hartwell's announcement.

Murmurs above her head reached vaguely through the cloudy thoughts that roamed her mind.

"He is so extremely handsome, don't you think?"

He had ever been so, and he had changed little—if she had been in any condition to judge. A dashing red-coat, who had returned her deep regard—inexplicably! Many had been her rivals, and no one had been more surprised than Annabel when he had sought her out.

"And so like Rebecca. There can be no doubt of his being her father."

No doubt at all. And so everyone must suppose who saw him. Oh, she was undone indeed!

A faint protesting sound escaped her, and the two ladies immediately bent towards her.

"Poor Annabel, are you a little recovered?"

She turned her eyes on Charlotte Filmer's anxious features. "I think I shall never recover."

"Oh, don't say so!" exclaimed Jane Emerson. "You are shocked, of course, and have not yet had time to realise—"

She was cut off with unusual curtness by the gentle Mrs Filmer. "Hush, Miss Emerson! She has time enough for realisation. Dear Annabel, take one little step at a time, I urge you. To be so suddenly re-united with your husband must be a severe disorientation.''

''Oh, yes, and he clearly saw it,'' agreed Jane eagerly. ''It shows such delicacy of feeling in Captain Lett to have brought Mr Hartwell to pave the way.''

Captain Lett! She had forgotten. Hal had come here posing as her husband, revoking her pretended widowhood. She was not ruined, but rather vindicated—but by a further lie. And one which gave him rights he did not have!

Abruptly, the implications of his action leaped into her mind. A surge of warmth overtook her as a memory—long thrust away as too painful to be contemplated—burst into life.

That little summerhouse! She had gone there, dragged by his impatient hand, only to indulge in a quarrel so empassioned that the deep-seated emotions that had bound them together had flamed, disastrously consuming them both.

Annabel had not blamed him for it, though he had bitterly condemned himself. She had been as much at fault, had owned as much to Papa. Only—

Her chest locked as the long-buried hurt rushed

up to taunt her. Only Captain Henry Colton, in whom she had believed so implicitly, had failed her. And now—more than three years too late!—he dared to return in a mockery of that role he should rightly have assumed at the outset, *as her husband*.

Wrath burned as she recognised how he had trapped her. Before three witnesses, no less. It would be all over the area before the cat could lick her ear! Useless to beg her friends to keep silent. They would, if she required it, she knew. But to what avail?

Mrs Amelia Hartwell was probably already in possession of the news. From the vicar's wife to the world was but a short step. And what hope had she of hiding anything when Aggie Binns was living not one hundred yards from her own door?

All vestige of that earlier shock had left her, replaced by fury such as Annabel had not felt in years. At his arrogance. At his sheer audacity!

Gripped by impatience, she rose abruptly. ''I must thank you both for your kindness. Will you think me rude if I ask you to leave me now?''

Her voice was shaking, and Jane instantly picked up on it.

''My dear Annabel, you are in no condition to be left alone!''

"Indeed, my dear, I am persuaded you ought to lie down upon your bed for a little," added the anxious Charlotte.

It was only by a supreme effort of will that Annabel prevented herself from shouting at them to go. But the habit of these last years reasserted itself. She was used now to suppressing the volcano of her feelings! She managed to summon a smile.

"Truly, I am over the shock now. But you will understand that the situation demands a degree of privacy." Her tone became vibrant, despite that tight control. "I must speak with Hal alone!"

"Hal? How charmingly that suits him!" exclaimed Jane Emerson.

Annabel could have screamed. It was plain that her friend had been carried away by the romance of it all. Well, if she was determined to approve the bogus Captain Lett, let her do so. She might sing another tune if she knew the truth!

To Annabel's relief, Charlotte Filmer intervened. "Come, Miss Emerson, we must take our leave. There must be so much to be said, and we are abominably *de trop.*'

Even as she spoke, the two gentlemen were seen to be returning around the corner of the house. The sight of Hal in person threw Annabel back into a degree of disorder, so that she scarcely took in the varied remarks of the well-wishers through the leave-taking. Yet in no time at all the murmur of voices died away, and she was left standing under the overhang of the chestnut tree, confronting a ghost from the past.

The silence lengthened. Hal knew not what to say. Almost he wished he had taken the sage warnings of his brother to heart. His determination, in the face of the apparent stranger that Annabel Howes had become, seemed to him now the product of that reckless temperament Ned had so often deprecated.

Regret his hastiness he might, but having taken this fatal step, he would stand buff. Only how to open communications with the creature he now faced utterly defeated him.

He drew a breath. "I have taken you by surprise."

An abrupt spurt of mirthless laughter escaped Annabel's lips. "To say the least."

Hal stiffened. "It was meant for the best."

Sudden fire from the green eyes took him aback. Annabel—much more the Annabel he remembered!—threw back her head, thrusting a defiant chin into the air.

"It was meant, Captain *Colton*, to ensure my acquiescence. It has not been so long that I am unable to recall your skill with tactics."

Hal let out a reluctant laugh. "The devil! And I thought you'd changed beyond recognition."

Annabel's fire died, and she tried to recover her rapidly slipping control. It was like a nightmare. Standing here in his presence, hearing his voice, a prey to every outraged feeling he had ever made her feel, so that she knew not what to feel or think. She barely knew that she answered him.

"I have changed, yes. Circumstance has a way of making one do so."

"So I see."

He received a bleak look that struck him between the ribs. Her voice had taken on coldness. She blamed him for the change! Why would she not? Guilt rose up. He took a pace towards her.

Annabel drew back. "Keep your distance! You need not imagine that your usurped identity gives you any rights concerning me."

Despite himself, Hal felt his temper rising. "What do you take me for? I have no intention of—"

"I am glad you chose to bring up the subject of your intentions, sir, because I am excessively interested to know what they might be."

Hal found it necessary to set his teeth against unwise utterance. He tried for a calmer note. "Annabel—"

She cut him short again. "Mrs Lett to you, sir."

"Oh, the devil!" he snapped, exasperated. "I am supposed to be your husband."

"Not by any will of mine."

"That I concede."

Annabel put a hand to her forehead, kneading it painfully. This could not be happening. If only she could think straight! She felt as if she had lost command of both her reason and her tongue. She did not want to bandy words with him. She wanted to fly across the intervening grass and batter at him with her fists! How dared he come here like this? How dared he presume so far? He, whose perfidy had brought her to this pass.

"I cannot talk to you," she managed, her hand falling to her side. "There is too much confusion—too much pain."

Hal watched her move unsteadily to the bench and sink down upon it. Compunction seized him. What had he done? Blundering in upon an ill-considered impulse. Devil take it, Ned had been right! He had taken an extreme measure that suited his own conscience, without thought to what distress it might cause at the other end.

Yet one thing spurred him. The short glimpse of that Annabel of his memories. She lay dormant, perhaps, but she was there. She had survived!

He dared to approach within a couple of paces of the figure that sat with bowed head, one hand pressed below her breast where an agitated motion was visible.

"Annabel."

Her eyes opened, and she looked up at him. Her eyes were dim with incomprehension. Her voice was an anguished whisper.

"How could you serve me so?"

Hal shifted his big shoulders uncomfortably. "I acted without thinking it through. I thought you would refuse even to see me, let alone allow me to make reparation."

The expression in her eyes became bleaker still. "Reparation. Is that what you came for?"

He dropped back a pace. "I came to take on responsibility for my actions. It is what I would have done a long time ago, as you must very well know."

Annabel's confusion deepened. "Must I? I have lived three years and more without knowing it!"

Hal stared at her for a moment, more puzzled than angry. "Oh, this must be to punish me. You cannot accuse me of deserting you, Annabel. It was you who vanished without trace. My regiment was posted away, it's true, but—''

She thrust a hand up to stop him. ''Pray do not make me any pretence of this kind. It is more than I can endure.''

He frowned deeply. But the solution leaped to the eye. ''I see your father's hand in this.''

At that she flared again. ''Don't dare speak hardly of my father! He has done more for me than you would have done.''

''Sending you here? What sort of a life is this?'' He waved an impatient hand. ''But let that pass. You wrong me, Annabel. I see what it is. Even in this extremity, your father would not unbend from that haughty arrogance that first parted us.''

Annabel got up abruptly. ''It was not my father who took me in the summerhouse that night!''

Hal's hot temper flared. ''You need not taunt me! Do you suppose I have not suffered agonies of remorse? Do you think I have not tried by every means in my power to make amends? Devil take it, Annabel! Have I no honour in your eyes?''

''Is it honour then that has brought you here today?''

She strode restlessly away across the grass,

moving in a jerky fashion that spoke clearly the agitation of her spirits. In movement and in voice, she resembled more and more the woman of Hal's remembrance. But her words pricked him.

"It is precisely that! I wronged you, and I have wanted ever since to right you in the eyes of the world."

Annabel turned on him. "Indeed? And so you have chosen to do so by ensuring that I live with you in sin!"

Hal's indignation deserted him. This aspect of the matter had not occurred to him. He lifted his fingers and smoothed at his moustache.

It was a characteristic gesture, and a shaft of affectionate memory gave Annabel a sensation as of melting. Just so had he always stood, caressing the short red hairs, whenever he had been disconcerted.

"Well, no one knows that," he said, recovering. "And once we are truly married—"

"How?" struck in Annabel. "When we are thought to be already married?"

He worked on his moustache for a moment or two in silence. Then he flung up a hand in a hopeless gesture.

"I had not thought of all this. You will think me a fool, I suppose. But the truth is that when I heard of your predicament, I acted instantly upon the knowledge with no thought for the consequences.''

Yes, it had been ever his way, she remembered. Then the substance of his remarks penetrated. ''How did you hear of it? Did you go to my father? No, he would not have told you!''

Hal pounced. ''Aha, you see! I knew he had thwarted me.''

But Annabel's gaze was accusing. ''How did you know?''

''I set a man to find you. He was here for some days not long since. He discovered not only your whereabouts, but your circumstances too. He thought you were a widow, but I remembered that Lett was your mother's name, and I knew it wasn't so. That is why I came.''

But the realisation that Captain Colton had spied upon her was the crowning insult. Her voice shook.

''You took too much upon yourself, sir. You think you have out-jockeyed me, but you are mistaken. A man may be seen to return from the dead, I grant you. But he may equally be seen to be recalled to his regiment! And that, Captain *Lett*, is precisely what is going to happen.''

With which, she turned on her heel and left him flat, heading for the rear of the little cottage.

Sleep eluded Annabel, despite a deadness of sensation that consumed her body. It had been a fatiguing day. When she had escaped from Hal, she had found herself so plagued by conflicting emotions that she had run past Janet and her daughter in the kitchen, startling them both, and had fled upstairs to indulge in a hearty bout of weeping.

This had proved so efficacious that she had been able at length to descend again, determined to present Captain Colton with a list of distinct rulings by which he might remain for a short time in his usurped status. In this she had been immediately balked on discovering from Janet that Hal had departed with Mr Hartwell, who had apparently waited for him.

"Gone? He has gone—and without a word said?"

"He'll be back, he said," the maid had responded, adding in the curt way habitual to her, "It's him, isn't it?"

Annabel had sighed out the abrupt sensation of renewed shock that had attacked her, and had plonked down on the sofa. Rebecca had promptly climbed into her lap, and Annabel had received her automatically, her eyes on Janet's thin-lipped disapproval.

"He's calling himself Captain Lett."

Janet had snorted. "And where are we to put him, ma'am, if I may make so bold?"

Annabel had flushed. "You need not set your imagination to work, Janet! You had best make up the truckle bed in the back room."

The maid had sniffed. "If I can set aside the bits and bobs of your sewing tackle."

This had been speedily dealt with. "Put them in my room for the time being."

Annabel had not doubted of its being only the first of the many inconveniences occasioned by the advent of a man into the little cottage. She had appropriated the smaller room behind the parlour for use as a workroom, ostensibly for the purpose of sewing clothes for herself and the infant, and for Janet too. But having begun by taking in a little mending to help a friend, Annabel had gradually acquired a small circle of clients among the more needy of the local ladies for whom she fashioned gowns, often out of old ones which she refurbished in the current mode. It was not an occupation that she cared to advertise. However, both Charlotte and Jane had used her services, along with others of the Guarding teachers and a gossipy spinster in Abbot Giles by the name of Lucinda Beattie.

It had been imperative to Annabel to conceal this activity from Hal. She did not wish him to think her reduced to such straits. Bad enough that she must tolerate his hateful condescension. He had come to make reparation indeed!

By the time he had returned, driving his own phaeton, and bringing with him a batman—whom Janet immediately stigmatized as the Jack-at-warts she had encountered hanging about the village green not long since—the light was fading and Rebecca had been long abed. Annabel, having resented Hal's arrival, had been for several hours in a fume at his prolonged absence.

"Since you left word you would come back, it would have been a courtesy in you to have said what time we might expect you," she had complained angrily.

"I couldn't because I didn't know," Hal had responded briefly, his bulk dwarfing even the large family room of Annabel's cottage.

Since it offered the most space, she had furnished it both with a sofa and one chair about the fireplace and a dining-table next to the window. A judiciously placed screen shut off the draught from the front door, which opened directly on to the room. So used to its inconvenient restrictions was Annabel that she no longer noticed them. Until tonight, when Captain Colton's appearance had made her all too aware of the shortcomings of her accommodation.

Balked of her complaint, she had sought another weapon with which to belabour him. "If you are expecting dinner, you will be disappointed, for we ate hours ago."

"I had a bite at the Hartwells before I left."

Annabel's frustration had deepened. "Janet says you have a man with you. Where you expect us to put him, I'm sure I don't know."

"Oh, I've arranged for that," Hal had announced, infuriatingly offhand. "He's to put up at a farm nearby, along with the phaeton and horses. I knew you could not have stabled them. And it was imperative that Weem remain with them, for I value my cattle too highly to leave them in charge of a farmhand."

There had been a pause. In the light of the few candles Annabel had left burning in one small candelabra, Hal's blue-grey eyes had glinted down at her from his superior height. Annabel's had met them defiantly, almost daring him to ask the question that hovered between them.

"Where have you put me?"

She had felt her colour rush up. "I dare say you will find it excessively uncomfortable."

Hal had smiled grimly. "I'm a soldier, Annabel. I'll sleep on the floor in the kitchen, if need be."

Annabel had swept to one side, avoiding his gaze. "We are not reduced to quite that extremity. Janet will show you the room." Without looking at him, she had offered grudgingly, "If you are hungry, I dare say she can find you bread and cheese, or some such thing."

He had refused it, and Annabel had murmured a gruff good night and escaped, leaving Janet to see to his needs. After she had heard the maid take herself to bed in the small room adjoining Becky's, Annabel yet could not sleep.

The unseen presence below stairs seemed to pervade the house, and her wandering thoughts were distressing enough to keep her wakeful. Inevitably, they drifted back to that fateful night at that last fashionable ball...

Without meaning it, her eyes had strayed automatically to every scarlet coat, discarding each broad-shouldered back as she did not find the familiar red-gold hair above it. In the event, Hal had found her instead. A touch on her shoulder, and as she turned, the familiar rush of warmth engulfed her as she encountered his serious gaze.

''I must speak with you alone!''

The low tone was anguished, and Annabel longed to give in. But in honour bound, she protested, her voice equally muted.

''To what avail, Hal?''

''Come with me, Annabel, I beg of you!''

He grasped her arm. Resistless, she allowed herself to be drawn through the motley crowds and out at the French windows. He took her hand, and pulled her across the terrace.

''For heaven's sake, Hal! If anyone were to see us!''

Hal's hurrying pace did not waver. ''There's a summerhouse of sorts. We can talk there.''

Her heart was beating like a drum, and Annabel knew she ought to turn back. But so dearly had she longed to see him again that she could not fight the impulse that drove her to match swift steps to his.

Night swallowed them up as the light that spilled on to the terrace fell further behind them. Hal slowed, guiding her silently across the grass. A shadow loomed ahead, and Annabel found herself stepping up into an arboured place, of circular structure, lit only by the stars and a splatter of moonlight thrusting through a patterned fretwork to lie unevenly upon the flagged floor.

Breathless, and not altogether from the chase, Annabel felt herself released. She shifted away from the large silhouette that was her discarded love, her pulses in riot. She broke into shaky speech.

"Why have you brought me here? There is nothing to be said between us, Hal. It is finished."

She could hear his uneven breath, and knew that his tempestuous nature was aroused.

"Yes, so you said a week ago. I was too upset, too angry to think then, Annabel. But I've had time enough since. You acted under your father's commands, I know it."

"Under his guidance," she corrected. "How could I marry you when he is so much opposed to it?"

"Even when his opposition is dictated by unreasoning obstinacy?"

Her eyes were growing accustomed to the dark, and Hal's big frame was becoming more visible. His nearness was torture to her. Yet she must adhere to that resolve that had driven her to reject him.

"Hal, we have had all this out. I am his only

child. It is natural that he should wish a better future for me than—''

''Than is to be had with a younger son who has only just acquired a captaincy,'' he finished bitterly. ''Don't tell me it again, for I don't believe it! Mr Howes knows well that I am a full-pay officer with a promising future.''

''He will not have me follow the drum, Hal.''

''If you don't care for that, why should he?''

''If Papa had forbidden me, or had treated me badly over this, I would not have hesitated,'' she uttered, low-voiced. ''He has tried instead to overcome his scruples—''

''Scruples!'' burst from Hal. ''His unreasoning prejudice rather.''

''Nothing of the sort. I assure you, he tried to hide his disappointment from me, but I could see his unhappiness. It was that which has been my undoing.''

''Emotional blackmail!'' scoffed Hal.

''Don't say that! How dare you say that? Papa would never use me so. He allowed our betrothal. It is I who chose to break it off. How can you abuse him?''

Hal gave a laugh in which bitterness sounded. ''With ease, Annabel. My darling, he is using your affection for him, don't you see? He may have given his consent against his will, but he gave it! And you have allowed him to twist you away from your own heart."

"Oh, stop!" cried Annabel, thrusting away as far as the small space would allow. "This is all so useless! Why can you not see how you hurt me with this persistence?"

"And what of my hurt, Annabel? I love you!"

Her heart twisted. "Don't, Hal!"

He moved swiftly, catching at her shoulders and pulling her to face him. "I must! Annabel, there is so little time. I can't leave England, knowing that you care for me, only to be tortured every moment by the thought of you marrying someone else."

Annabel tried to drag away. "Let me go! Can't you see that you are pulling me in half? Hal, this is so unfair! Do you think it cost me nothing to reach that decision? I love you too, but—"

"That's all I wanted to hear!" he said gutturally.

Next instant, Annabel found herself jerked against his broad chest as his mouth sought hers. Warmth flooded her, and for a moment she clung to him, answering the hunger of his lips with a desire as fervid as his own.

But the image of Papa's distressing upset thrust

rudely into her mind. She wrenched back, the force of her motion breaking his hold.

"You must not! Hal, for heaven's sake, let me be! I cannot marry you. I cannot!"

He did not pursue her as she backed away, but his ragged breath gave her audible evidence of his unabated passion. It had the opposite effect to the one she ought to experience. She could feel her limbs trembling, and a desperate yearning opened up in those hollows that she knew to be most vulnerable to his need.

"You belong with me, Annabel. This is ruining both our lives, and you know it. And for what? For the ravings of an obstinate devil, who is so eaten up with prejudice that he sacrifices the happiness of his own daughter!"

Annabel flew at him then, her hands curled into fists. She tried to hit at him, raging.

"Be silent! Beast! Brute! How I hate you!"

He had caught her wrists, holding them fast.

"Wildcat! Stop it!"

But Annabel was crying with rage, and her protests became the more vehement. She knew not what she said, only that she wanted to kill him for hurting her so...

How it had happened, Annabel had never afterwards been able to recall. Even now, wakeful in her bed, all this time later. But she had found herself lying upon the flagged stone of the summerhouse, in a tangle of legs and panting breath, with the man who slept tonight in the room below.

And when Hal, coming for an instant to his senses, would have stopped it, Annabel was guiltily aware that she had been the one so lost in love and desire who had plunged them back into that total consummation.

Only afterwards, as she lay in his arms, her mind hazy with fulfilment, had the enormity of the proceeding gradually seeped into her consciousness.

Hal had cursed himself with a will. But Annabel, horrified by the realisation of what had happened, had begged him to go and alert her coachman that she might make a hurried and unseen exit from the ball.

He had done as she wished, and by the time he had returned, Annabel had been too overwrought to listen to anything he may have said. She could remember nothing of his words, although she knew that he had addressed her in tones of earnest agitation as he had escorted her to the coach.

What she did remember was the tearful confession she had poured into Papa's ears. He had been distressed, but not angry—not then. But he had hustled her out of town that very night, and into the country. A tale had been put about by the lady who was sponsoring her that she had been taken suddenly ill, but Annabel had no means of knowing whether it had been believed.

She had not been seen in fashionable circles since. Like the fictitious Captain Lett, Annabel Howes had disappeared without trace. And until he had thrust himself back into her life this afternoon in her little garden in Steep Ride, Annabel had neither heard from nor set eyes on Captain Colton from that night.

Chapter Three

In the small ground-floor room, Captain Colton lay as wakeful as his reluctant fictitious spouse. He had thrust the casement open as far as it would go, but it was still stuffy. The truckle bed could scarcely be said to accommodate his large frame with any degree of ease, but it was not this discomfort that was keeping sleep at bay. He had been in far worse situations, and had slept like the dead—or so Weem claimed. But he had much to ponder.

He had set himself a task that looked likely to prove well-nigh impossible. There was little of the Annabel he had been pursuing in the creature who had accorded him such resentful acceptance this day. Acceptance? It could scarce be called that! Had he not carried out his plan of campaign, she would certainly have thrown him out.

Whether he was glad of having done it was another question entirely. He had thought—naïvely, he was forced now to admit—that the feeling he had for Annabel would be with him unto death. Certainly the intervening years had done nothing to dim its strength.

But in ruthless honesty, Hal conceded that it had been dealt a severe blow by his first sight of the stranger Annabel this afternoon. Had he driven himself through battles and arduous campaigns in Spain and Portugal, holding her image sacred in a determined bid to win her in the end, only to find at the last that he had mistaken his own heart?

Where was the girl who had given herself to him in the torrid heat of mutual passion when last he had seen her? Had he carried a false picture of that night, building in his imagination upon the actuality so that he cherished an exaggerated memory? The sequel he remembered all too well.

Returning distraught to his lodgings, he had discovered orders to rejoin his regiment in Dover the next day, from there to embark at once for Spain. He had chased like a demented fool in the early hours to the Howes town residence, only to find the knocker off the door and the shutters up. A sleepy retainer had been roused at last to his

furious banging, from whom he had learned that
the master was gone out of town.

There had been nothing he could do but write—
letter after letter. And for months nothing had
come. He had thought that Annabel was punishing
him by her silence. Until the letters came back in
a package, unopened except for the first. That had
been torn in two.

For a while Hal had given up. But when nearly
a year had gone, his heart as desperate as ever, he
had again written. And the letter came back with
its seal intact. After that, he must now suppose,
Annabel had been established here in this village.
Had he written, she would probably not have received the letters.

From her hasty words today, he must suppose
that she never had received them. Howes had
played him false! No doubt leading Annabel to
suppose that he had never made any attempt to
contact her. Small wonder that she had reacted to
his arrival with resentment.

He must show her the letters. At the least let
her not think him basely treacherous.

Only that seed of doubt lingered. Hal wished
he had not been so hasty. If Annabel no longer
loved him—if he, let it be said, could not love the
woman she had become—then of what use was

his presence here? Perhaps he ought, after all, to pretend that he had been recalled to his regiment. It had been Annabel's suggestion. Thrown at him in anger it was true, yet it had merit.

His arrival would establish her respectability in the neighbourhood. He would meet his obligations, whatever happened, with any financial aid Annabel thought proper. He might remain a few weeks, put on a pretence of familial harmony, and withdraw again with no harm done.

His hardened honesty gave him a mental kick. No harm done! Was there not harm enough in his throwing Annabel back into an episode in the past which he had no doubt at all she had done her best to forget? No, he must face it. He had compounded his original fault by appearing in this way.

On this painful thought, he began to drop asleep, a half-formed resolve in his mind to talk bluntly to Annabel the following day, and assure her that he intended to withdraw from the vicinity as soon as was decently possible.

In the morning, however, in search of hot water with which to wash and shave, he blundered sleepily into the large room, looking for the kitchen, dressed only in shirt and breeches. Here he encountered a small child playing on the floor.

The infant was dressed in a nightgown, and a pair of large blue eyes regarded him solemnly out of an adorable little face surrounded by a mass of curling locks that matched almost exactly the colour of his own.

Hal's heart lurched. The babe! A girl? Devil take it, why had no one said it was a little girl? Something seemed to kick him in the chest. *His daughter*. This was his daughter!

The child continued to gaze up at him, the wooden horse and cart motionless under her still hands. She did not appear to be afraid. Hal dropped to his haunches.

"Hello! What's your name?"

At that, she looked coyly, and one small hand reached up to her mouth, slipping a finger inside.

Before Hal could repeat his question, the gaunt woman who seemed to be Annabel's only servant appeared in the doorway behind. Her gaze was anything but friendly, her tone sour.

"Her name's Rebecca."

The infant removed the finger from her mouth, and piped up. "Becca."

"She can't say it right, so we call her Becky mostly."

Hal smiled at the child, and held out his hand. "How do you do, Becky?"

His daughter looked at the hand, and back up to his face. Then she scrambled up, and ran to embrace the dour maid's legs.

"She'll be shy of you to start with, sir," volunteered the maid, leaning down to pick up the child.

Hal rose. "No doubt."

The woman clearly knew his identity. And strongly disapproved of him, if he was any judge. He changed his tone to one of command.

"I'll be glad of some hot water, if it isn't too much trouble."

Annabel's clear voice spoke from the stairway to one side. "It is a great deal too much trouble. Janet has enough to do without fetching water. You'll find a tin jug on the stove in the kitchen."

She came down the stairs. Without glancing at Hal, she went to Janet and took Rebecca. "I'll see to her. Has she had breakfast?"

"No, ma'am. There's eggs on the boil. I'll show the Captain his water, and then bring them in."

Hal thanked her, and followed her through the doorway, glancing once at the little girl as he went. A warm glow filled his breast. Hardly did he notice the reflection that passed through the

back of his mind. That the resolve he had made
in the night had been abruptly shattered.

By the time Hal had performed his ablutions,
there was no sign in the house of either Annabel
or Rebecca. He was requested to sit at the table
in the window where a cover had been set for him,
and was regaled with eggs and ham by the grudg-
ing maid. She informed him, upon enquiry, that
the mistress was gone out.

"To church perhaps?"

He received a look that would have been in-
solence in any subordinate of his. "It'll be a while
yet before she does that now, sir."

It was said with meaning, and Hal gritted his
teeth. The implication was plain. Now that her
alleged husband was home, it would be thought
odd indeed if the "Letts' did not attend church as
a family. Hal guessed that the Reverend Mr
Hartwell would assume Annabel to be yet too
much overcome by his arrival to be at service today. It struck him—not without a degree of self-
blame—that it would have been hard indeed for
Annabel to confront the inevitable gossip.

"Where is she then?" he asked of the maid.

Was that thin smile one of satisfaction? Had the
wretched woman fathomed his discomfiture?

"She'll be tilling the soil in the vegetable patch, sir."

"*What?*"

"Or gathering up some produce. I'm not much for planting myself, but I think it's too early for seeding."

Hal did not bother to hide his feelings. He guessed it had been said to taunt him, but he was too upset to care. To what was Annabel reduced? To what depths of drudgery had he condemned her? Had she so little money at her disposal that she must forage for food like a pauper?

The meal abruptly turned his stomach, and he laid down his knife and fork with a clunk.

The maid tutted. "Waste not, want not."

Hal gave her a look that had made strong men quail. "Don't try me too far!"

The woman was not flustered. She gave him back look for look, placing her arms akimbo. "I know what I know, but I've stood by her, Captain." She nodded at his plate. "And it might be otherwise in the army, but we don't waste food. Not in this house!"

It was touch and go for an instant, but then Hal's sense of humour came to the fore. He relaxed, smiling a little.

"I see that Mrs Lett is lucky to have you. What is your name?"

"Janet, sir. And you needn't think you can worm your way around me!"

"I don't," said Hal cheerfully. "But if we're to be at outs, Janet, let it be in the open." He took up his knife and fork again. "However, you need not imagine I intend to add to your burden of work. I can fend for myself, and I'll do my share as long as I'm here."

It was plain that he had disconcerted the maid, but she eyed him suspiciously. "As long as when?"

"That I don't yet know."

For a moment or two, the woman was silent while Hal ate. Then she sniffed, losing some of her acerbity.

"We've a boy comes in to do the heavy work. Lazy he is, if you don't watch him. But there's no need I can see for you to bestir yourself."

Hal gave her a grim look. "Think of me as you choose, Janet, but wait and learn." He reached for the coffee-pot and filled his cup. "If you want to serve Mrs Lett, you can tell me just what the situation is as regards income."

Janet drew herself up. "The mistress can tell you all you need to know."

"But she won't."

"Then I won't neither," asserted Janet, folding her arms. "But if you want my say-so, that there curmudgeon has behaved shabby to her, and no mistake!"

Taking this to refer to old Mr Howes, Hal nodded as he dug a fork into a chunk of ham. "More shabbily than you are aware of, I suspect, Janet."

He received a disparaging snort in reply. "And you're the one to say so, Captain!"

Hal glanced up, his mouth full. "If you mean by that to imply that I have behaved shabbily, you're telling me nothing I don't already know."

This was subjected to an even more comprehensive snort. "And I don't doubt you'll use the same means of turning her up sweet an' all!"

With which, the woman turned towards the kitchen. Retreating upon the point of fraternising with the enemy? Hal stopped her nevertheless.

"One moment. Just where is this vegetable patch, if you please?"

He had not far to look. From the back entrance to End Cottage, one could go two ways. To the garden situated to one side where he had first encountered Annabel yesterday. Or, in the opposite direction, to a much larger area, fenced off high with hedging all around and entirely given over to planting.

Hal could see several fruit trees, a collection of climbing peas or beans supported by a cane fretwork, and rows of beds, plentifully stocked with a variety of greenery. From lean times on the Peninsula, Hal was familiar with the look of certain growing vegetables. Many a Spanish farmer had he been obliged to compensate for the ravaging of his stocks by hungry troops. Often enough he had entered into negotiations with locals, haggling over a few straggly turnips to enhance a meagre broth.

It might have been these experiences that caused a surge of passionate indignation to rise up in him when he spied not only Annabel on her knees, but his little daughter too, jabbing into the earth with spade and fork.

"This is intolerable!"

Annabel jumped, quickly turning her head. The sight of Captain Colton's large person posed threateningly in the middle of her kitchen garden threw a shaft of dismay into her breast. It was swiftly succeeded by a rise of that resentment which she had not yet had an opportunity to discharge.

She sat back on her haunches, lifting her chin,

the fork poised in mid-air. "What is the matter? Are you shocked to see a gently bred female thus engaged? If you mean to remain here, you will have to accustom yourself to such sights."

"I am shocked to realise the extent of your father's malice. That he should have condemned you to this!" Hal swept an arc with his hand that was meant to encompass the whole of her life.

"Instead of exposing me to the rigours of following the drum with a campaigning army?" countered Annabel. "Between you, I had little to choose."

Hal compressed his lips upon a sharp retort. It had not been his intention to provoke her. Instead, he glanced to where Rebecca, with concentrated attention, had returned to her task of shovelling earth from a growing hole. A pink tongue protruded between her lips as she hefted the spade, which was over-large for her small hands, and dribbled the small load it contained on to a pile to one side of the bed being worked.

Her errant father's disapproval was not lost on Annabel. Her voice took on sarcasm. "Child labour. It is never too early to start when one's future is going to depend upon one's own efforts."

She received a look that chilled her, and his tone was gruff. "That was uncalled for."

Annabel felt herself falling into remorse, and quickly rallied. "As was your untimely appearance upon the scene in the guise of my dead husband."

Hal toyed with the tempting notion of dragging her up from the grass where she sat and shaking her until the teeth rattled in her head. That, or turning abruptly from her and kicking the dust of this place from his heels! Regretfully, either course was ineligible. He knew he had bought into this, and must take the consequences. It would not help to give rein to his unruly temper. He drew in his horns.

"When you are free, I would appreciate an opportunity to discuss our situation."

"*Your* situation. It has been none of my creating."

"Devil take it, Annabel, come down off your high ropes! May we not call a truce?"

The exasperation in his voice had startled Rebecca into dropping her shovel. She began instantly to cry.

"Now see what you've done!"

But Annabel's attention shifted quickly to her daughter. It had not been, she at once guessed, the loud voice that had upset the child, but the consequent ruin of her careful efforts. Rebecca was notoriously sensitive concerning any little task she undertook. She would tolerate neither interference nor destruction in any part of what she had achieved.

The earth had scattered, spoiling the neatness of her arrangements. It did not matter that her own unsteady hand had left a trail between the hole and the dirt pile, for that was part of the pattern. But her complaints, which were largely unintelligible through her sobs, evidently encompassed that area which had been dirtied by the little accident, for her small fists were beating at the ground.

"Come now, Becky, that is enough!" said Annabel with authority. "See, I will clean it for you, and it will be as good as ever."

But it was not until the little girl could indeed recognise the truth of this assertion, as Annabel hurriedly gathered up as many of the scattered fragments back into the shovel as she could prise from the grass, that Rebecca's lamentations abated.

Hal watched with tenderness at his heart as Annabel placed his daughter's fingers about the shovel and helped her to empty its contents on to the proper pile. Rebecca consented then to have the ravages of her tantrum wiped away, and became once again absorbed as Annabel tucked the handkerchief back into a pocket of her faded gown.

"She would appear to have inherited more than my colouring," commented Hal amusedly.

Caught off guard, Annabel smiled, rising to her feet. "She has the devil's own temper, it is true. But I believe I must share in the blame for that."

She looked at him as she spoke, and a certain warmth in the blue-grey eyes as they rested upon her sent a flitter down her pulses. For an instant or two, she could not look away.

Then the recollection of her wrongs rose up into her mind, and she broke the contact, finding occupation in brushing the dirt from her fingers. She moved a little away from her daughter, lowering her voice.

"What did you wish to talk to me about?"

Hal was conscious of a sinking in his chest. For a brief moment, there had been an echo in the green eyes of the passion that had been responsible for the life so busily engaged in the vegetable bed. But Annabel had veiled it—if he had not imagined it! She looked again a very matron. The cotton gown donned for her work was old-fashioned and faded, and her dark hair was confined under a neat mob cap with a small frill.

Even in the casual neatness of his buckskins and the green frock-coat, she made Hal feel out of place.

He adopted as neutral a note as he could manage, choosing his words with care. "There are several matters, but I will begin with what I hope may lessen the problem I have saddled you with by coming here."

Annabel's gaze flew to his, a startled question in her eyes. "You are going away again?"

How disconcerting was her ability to outguess him! She was ever quick. Her sharp intelligence had been one of the characteristics that had attracted him at the outset. Yet he could not tell whether the notion was welcome to her.

"You said it yourself yesterday, Annabel. If need be, 'Captain Lett' can always be recalled to his regiment."

She looked him over, a hint of suspicion in her face. "But you are not wearing regimentals. And your scheme cannot have anticipated a recall. Have you sold out?"

A laugh compound of exasperation and amusement escaped Hal. "The devil fly away with you! Yes, I have."

Annabel waited for more, battening down upon a leap of hope in her breast that bore no relation to what was in her mind. He had taken a good deal for granted, she told herself rebelliously. And just when it suited him!

Aware of hostility in her, Hal tried for a non-chalance that he was far from feeling. "My god-father died. He was a friend of my father's and lived near the family estates. Perhaps you remember? He left me the house and lands. They are modest, but it has given me a reasonable competence."

"Enough to support your child, and the woman who bore her," suggested Annabel, deceptively mild.

Hal was not fooled. He drew a difficult breath. "You have a right to be angry. But I must and will set the record straight. I have all my letters to you, Annabel. Every one returned, unread except for the first."

A sweeping flame of anger took Annabel unawares. But it was not directed at Hal. If what he said was the truth, then Papa had used her more ill than she had known! Her distress and outrage were acute, but she held them tightly in. But there was nothing she could do about her thickening voice.

"Had you no letter from me?"

Hal shook his head, a fierce frown clouding his

brow. ''None. As you say you heard nothing from me, so did I have no word at all from you.''

Annabel could neither speak, nor look at him. Stumbling a little in her haste, she picked a way through the beds to the relatively clear spaces among the fruit trees, her chaotic thoughts dictating the pace of her feet.

Hal had written! He had tried to make amends. Papa must have concealed the letters from her, persuading her to believe at length that having made of her a wanton, Captain Colton no longer wanted to wed her. Rather than give her in marriage to a man against whom his mind was set, her father had preferred to place her within a living lie where penury was her unenviable lot. And it had been for his sake that Annabel had given up the man she loved!

The whole dreadful tangle of it choked her. Hal could have saved her. Rebecca could have been born in wedlock, her future assured under the care of her real father. She would have married him in love, unencumbered by the bitterness that now affected all her existence; that had been resurrected on the instant of seeing his face. Wrongly resurrected, as it chanced, for the blame was not Hal's, but her father's.

Hal had come, nevertheless, to rectify matters.

But this thought, instead of alleviating her distress, only increased the anguish. For it was all too late! What love she'd had for Hal had been destroyed by her belief of his perfidy. And from his demeanour she could not doubt that though he had come, it was not for love, but from a sense of duty.

"Annabel!"

She stopped dead in her tracks, but she did not look at him. Her heart was too full, the bitterness that had before been dormant now overwhelming. Oh, that he had not come!

With difficulty, she formulated words, only vaguely aware of the harsh flat sound with which they came out.

"If I have done you an injustice, there will be time enough for repentance."

Her manner threw Hal into as strong a resentment as she had earlier shown him. "If you do not believe me, I will show you the letters! I brought them on purpose that I might vindicate myself."

God, no! To read them would be more than she could endure. "It will not be necessary. I accept your word."

"I am honoured!"

The ironic inflection was not lost on Annabel.

But she was beyond mending what she had said. She was near to screaming. Only habit enabled her to speak with any degree of normality.

"Pray leave me. I need—a little time for reflection."

Hal hesitated for a space. Why could she not rail at him? It would have been preferable to this comprehensive withdrawal. He could not understand it. If she was ready to believe him, why had it not changed her attitude towards him? There was nothing he could usefully say.

"I will go, if you wish it."

She only nodded, neither looking at him, nor relaxing the stiff pose. But as he turned to go, she spoke again.

"Hal—"

It was the first time she had used his name. A pang smote him. He paused. "Yes?"

But there was no relenting on her part. "Pray ask Janet to come and watch Rebecca."

Hal almost offered to watch in the maid's place. Prudence, however, bade him do as she wished. The child might object to be given himself as a substitute. And Annabel clearly wanted him out of the way. He left her without another word.

Annabel listened to the sound of his footsteps, her eyes closing tight shut. She had no tears, for

her despair was too deep. But his departure gave
some little ease. His presence was altogether too
destructive to her peace of mind. It had been easier before.

Rather would she have continued to hold him
in that repressed hatred that had enabled her to
pretend she had forgot. The pretence had been for
her protection. How could she possibly forget?

Now it seemed that she must forgive. No, not
forgive, for there was no fault! She never had
blamed him for the deed. She was as much responsible, and had ever known it. It was only the
apparent sequel for which she had driven her love
into hatred. Even could she reverse it—impossible
task!—what would be the point? Hal plainly no
longer loved her. That much had been clear from
the moment of setting eyes upon him. Indeed, recalling the expression in his face at that first instant—which in her own shock she had been unable to take in at the time—she fancied she could
see revulsion!

No, Hal did not love her, nor she him. And she
would prefer to remember him with loathing than
to know that the feelings they had inspired in each
other had vanished without trace. What price
Rebecca then, who had been conceived in love?

It was not to be endured! She could not live in

a travesty of the dreams they once had shared. He must go. She would tell him so. Anything else was impossible.

Annabel listened with a sensation of dull despair to the chattering vivacity of her visitor. The youthful Lady Wyndham was fashionably attired in a charming gown of sprigged muslin and a light blue pelisse expensively adorned with ribbon and lace. She had carelessly discarded a frivolously feathered bonnet that threw an incongruous splash of crimson and blue upon Annabel's faded sofa. A riot of golden curls framed an exquisite countenance in which a pair of pansy eyes gave ample evidence of their owner's present happiness.

How delighted Annabel would have been to witness it only five days ago! But every word the Viscountess had to say only emphasised the contrast between their respective situations, and drove in deeper the leaden weight that had dogged her since Hal had arrived.

"...and I told George that I would by no means settle at Lyford Manor if he would not let me come first to Bredington on purpose to see you, dearest Annabel."

"I am flattered," Annabel managed, summoning a smile.

Lady Wyndham laughed. "Don't be, silly creature! Why, I shall never forget that I owe it to you that I was at last brought to my senses. And you assisted at my wedding. I shall always count you my friend, Annabel."

The appeal of the warm brown gaze could not be resisted, and a little of Annabel's reserve left her. Her intervention in the young lady's affairs had been incidental, but it was true that she had done her best to prevent her from ruining what little reputation had been left to her through no fault of her own, poor child. She reached across the dining-table where they were informally seated, and pressed the girl's hand.

"I am glad to have been of assistance, Lady Wyndham, especially since it is obvious that you are wildly happy."

"Oh, no, no!" exclaimed the young visitor, catching at the hand before Annabel could withdraw it. "I am ecstatic, it is true, but you must call me Serena. To be styled so formally by one and all is just the sort of stuffiness that I detest!" A giggle escaped her. "Indeed, I am a great trial to poor George upon occasion. Though I am quick to remind him that it was that very habit of mine of expressing myself without thinking that he protested he liked at the start."

Annabel had to smile. "I dare say that what might have been endearing in Miss Serena Reeth may not be acceptable in Lady Wyndham."

"Oh, yes, and it makes me out of reason cross!" agreed Serena gaily, making a face. "Indeed, it was what led to the most dreadful quarrel between us."

If there had been only one, she was indeed fortunate, thought Annabel, recalling with a hollowing at her stomach the dreadful consequences of that most serious quarrel between herself and Hal. But she quelled her thoughts and listened to Lady Wyndham's artless disclosures with an assumption of interest.

But when she understood that the basis of the quarrel had been a scandalous publication that had appeared early that year, she could not withhold her shocked surprise.

"What, you mean *The Wicked Marquis*? Serena! Surely you have not read that dreadful book? I know it must be of interest to all of us, being a parody of Sywell and his antics, but to my understanding, it is meant for gentlemen."

A choked giggle escaped Serena, and her eyes danced. "I know, and it is indeed shockingly unsuited for gently bred females—as Wyndham was swift to inform me."

Annabel was not surprised. There had been a deal of talk in the villages when it came out, and although no one in her own circle had seen a copy, rumour had it that the contents were disgracefully lewd. It had enjoyed a vogue among gentlemen. Not due to its style, but because of the satirical portraiture of the persons depicted therein. They were nearly all peers, and thinly disguised. Annabel knew that Viscount Wyndham had been one of them.

"What was I to do," Serena enjoined, "when Wyndham sat there laughing his head off and refused to tell me anything about it, except that Lord Buckworth had sent it to him?"

"That was ill done of him, I dare say, but—"

"Annabel, don't you turn stuffy on me!" protested Serena reproachfully. "I know it was naughty, but I sneaked a look at it, and found myself riveted. Especially when I realised that Lord Windyhead was meant for George. But he was furious with me for daring to read it, and—"

"Of course he was, and with reason," interrupted Annabel. "And you know it, Serena!"

The visitor blushed, and tossed her golden locks. "Yes, but it was quite Wyndham's own fault. He should have read it in private if he meant to keep it secret."

"I suppose you told him so?"

Serena nodded emphatically. "I did. And also that it would serve him out if I had believed the dreadful things it said of him. For you remember that I had been told George had been an intimate of Sywell's."

Annabel well remembered. She had been able to assure Serena that it was not so. "And did that reconcile him?"

"No, indeed," said Lady Wyndham, giggling again. "It sent him into a towering rage! Indeed, he said such things as I could not easily forgive. It was quite three days before I would talk to him again."

Three days! A pang smote Annabel. What price three years then? And Serena had not lost her husband's love over it.

"But you forgave each other in the end?"

The brown eyes sank into dreamy warmth. "Oh, yes. At last George said he could not endure to see me unhappy. I wept and wept, you know, for it was so horrid to be at outs with him. But to make amends, he took me to Venice, and bought me the prettiest fan imaginable—I wish I had brought it to show you, Annabel—and so all was forgotten at last."

Forgotten? And forgiven too. Oh, that her own life might be as simply rectified!

But Lady Wyndham's disclosures were not at an end. Numbly, Annabel took in the rest.

"It was soon after that I discovered I was increasing, and poor George became even more repentant." Her eyes lit again with laughter. "I may tell you, Annabel, that we nearly quarrelled all over again when my darling husband took it into his head to hedge me about with all manner of restrictions."

"Indeed? It is why you set off to come home, I imagine?"

"Oh, I don't mind that. But would you believe it? George is adamant that I may not re-enter society until after I am confined. I must remain quietly at Lyford Manor—though that will be no hardship, for my mama-in-law Lady Kettering is a delightful creature—and refrain from any undue exertion. I may not dance, nor ride—oh, all manner of things. It is utterly ridiculous, and so I told him."

Ridiculous it may have been, but it contrasted so ill with Annabel's own pregnancy that she could barely repress a moan of despair. She had been as much restricted, but upon the point of secrecy, not care of her well-being. There had been no anxious husband for Annabel!

"I forgive him only because he confided that he is so much afraid of losing me," disclosed Serena, with a look so smug to Annabel's eyes that it was with difficulty that she refrained from slapping her friend.

She delivered herself a mental kick, and thrust into speech, almost unknowing what she said.

"I am sure there is no need for him to fear for you. You are young and healthy, and I am sure Lady Kettering will see that you are guided by the best physicians."

"Oh, yes," agreed Serena blithely. "I am not at all concerned. Though I was very sick for the first week or two. But that has happily passed off, and aside from fatigue from the journey, I never felt better in my life."

"You are fortunate," said Annabel mechanically. "I was unwell throughout."

Though that had not been due to her pregnancy, for the early nausea had vanished after a few weeks. Yet she had been almost constantly ailing, with unexplained aches and ills—the result, she had always believed, of the circumstances and the anxiety occasioned by the lack of response to her increasingly frantic letters to Hal.

She was obliged to give her attention to her guest again when Lady Wyndham began to talk of the death of the Marquis of Sywell, asking all manner of questions, and remarking upon the similarity of that occurrence to the sequence of events in the parody that had occasioned her quarrel with her husband. Glad of the change of subject, Annabel informed her of the latest development concerning Solomon Burneck's relationship to Sywell. She was just beginning to recover a little ease of manner when she found that Serena had fallen silent, and was eyeing her with expectancy.

Annabel frowned. "What is the matter?"

A grimace crossed Serena's lovely features. "Dear Annabel, are you not going to tell me your news? Here have I been waiting and waiting, chattering on about myself and hoping all the time that you will trust me enough to confide in me. But you say nothing, and so you force me to ask—is it true?"

There could be no mistaking the meaning of this. It was just as Annabel had feared. The news of her "husband's" return had already resulted in a number of little notes of congratulation from persons round about. And if Serena, who had only just returned to England, had heard it, the news must have travelled far afield.

"You refer, I collect, to Captain Lett's return?"

Serena's expression turned to doubt. "Why, Annabel, what is the matter? Is it not occasion for great happiness?"

Annabel tried, but she could not form either smile or words to reassure her guest. Her fingers drummed absently on the table as she strove for calm. To her consternation, Lady Wyndham's gaze became concerned.

"You are distressed! Oh, Annabel, what is it? Do you find that you do not love him any longer?"

Pain stabbed at Annabel's bosom, and tears sprang to her eyes. How was it that this innocent girl struck with uncanny accuracy at the root of her distress? With difficulty, she forced words through the tightness at her throat.

"It is—difficult. Three years! There are circumstances which…"

Her voice failed, and she felt Serena's warm fingers close over her own.

"Dearest Annabel, pray don't cry! I understand you, I believe. At least, I know what it is to be uncertain. But don't despair, I beg of you. There is time yet. At least you are together. You will have every opportunity of working it out between you."

A wavering smile crossed Annabel's lips. "Perhaps. Forgive me. I did not mean to distress you with…'

"Now that is silly! But you must be wishing me otherwise. Here have I been running on about my own delights, and all the time you have been miserable."

This was not to be borne. "No, no, Serena. I am very happy for you. Pray do not blame yourself."

But Lady Wyndham would have none of this. She got up from her chair and came around the table to give her hostess a convulsive hug.

"There! I will not press you to talk of it, but pray believe me when I tell you that I will be thinking of you with great affection. Write to me, Annabel, pray do! I will be anxious to hear." Her candid smile lit her face. "And you know how Wyndham is determined I shall not suffer the least anxiety. You must write to me, or I shall be obliged to send him here to find out your situation. Promise me now!"

Annabel found herself giving the required promise, if only to rid herself of the insidious guilt at inflicting her own troubles to shadow this young creature's happiness. In a flurry of affectionate good wishes, Lady Wyndham then retrieved her bonnet, and obliged Annabel to accompany her to the carriage which awaited her outside. Lord Wyndham, she disclosed, had categorically refused to allow her to ride the short distance from Bredington. Annabel had just submitted to a warm embrace, when Captain Colton himself drove up in his phaeton.

She stiffened, beset by an unreasoning sensation of jealous rage. For beside him, beaming with pleasure, sat little Miss Lett.

Chapter Four

Nothing could be said before the visitor, and in the face of Serena's expectant look, Annabel felt obliged to confirm his identity.

"That is he. Would you wish me to present him to you?"

"Pray do." Serena leant to whisper, a trifle of excitement in her tone. "He is excessively handsome, Annabel. Surely your affections cannot help but reanimate towards him!"

At this precise moment, Annabel's feelings towards him were anything but affectionate. She said nothing, however, merely awaiting the opportunity to make the necessary introduction.

His servant having leaped down from the perch behind and run to the horses' heads, Hal was already descending. He moved to lift Becky from the phaeton, but the little girl instantly pushed his hands away, shrieking her intention of staying exactly where she was.

"Oh, dear!" laughed Lady Wyndham. "I see that nothing has changed with her, though she has grown a good deal."

Annabel forced a laugh. "She is even more wilful, if anything."

"But she is so beautiful that no one will care. I only hope my own offspring may be as charming."

Her gaze returned to the carriage, into which the Captain had once more mounted and was seen to be conversing in low tones with his daughter, who had, as usual, divested herself of the bonnet that Annabel had seen her wearing when she had set off with Janet for her walk. The flame of her hair rioted about the little face, and it came as no surprise that Serena was moved to comment upon the similarity of colour.

"Though I fancy Becky's hair is a shade brighter," she concluded with interest.

"Hal's was once a stronger colour," responded Annabel without thinking. "Only he was used to tell me that it tended to fade under the hot Spanish sun."

By this time, it was to be seen that Hal had

somehow overcome Rebecca's recalcitrance, and had persuaded the child to vacate the phaeton. She nestled comfortably in his arms as he came towards the ladies. A very mite she looked against the relatively giant stature of her father. A shaft of anguish thrust through Annabel's bosom, depriving her momentarily of speech.

Fortunately, Serena chose to address herself immediately to the little girl, giving Annabel a moment or two to recover in time to perform the necessary introduction.

"Captain Lett, this is Lady Wyndham."

A few politenesses were exchanged before Serena bade them adieu and entered her carriage. In the general leavetaking, Annabel felt all the falsity of her situation. In particular because the lie in the apparent family group was to her an abuse of Lady Wyndham's avowed friendship.

As the carriage drove away and Hal turned to her, it was evident that he had divined her upset.

"You are displeased," he said flatly. "I beg your pardon. I saw Rebecca walking with Janet, and thought it might give her pleasure to be taken up beside me. If you had rather I did not do so again, you have only to say so."

Annabel was instantly torn by conflicting emotions. He had picked up the very thing that shamed her! Her first violent reaction of jealousy had been wholly inappropriate. Yet, with her conscience raw from the necessity to deceive Serena, this attack thrust her into an anger yet more inapposite to the circumstances. Especially since he chose to couch it in a travesty of an apology!

"Becky appears to have enjoyed it," she managed, aware that her tone belied the noncommittal words.

Since Rebecca chose this moment to embark upon an involved and lengthy description of her adventure, addressing herself to her mother, Hal was unable to answer.

He was glad of it, for the violence of the only response he felt able to give would have been entirely unacceptable! Yes, the child had enjoyed it enormously—as was evidenced by the excitement in her voice as she related the tale. But he was not fooled by Annabel's apparent acceptance. She was furious with him, that much he had seen at the outset.

To the devil with it all! There was to be no quarter, no matter what he did. These few days, since he had told her about the letters, she had been distant—almost to the point of hatred.

He had tried to remain unobtrusive in the management of the cottage, knowing full well that any interference would be taken in bad part. Much though the assistance he could readily render was needed!

In the first place, although the food that found its way to the table was well cooked and neatly presented, there was a lack of variety to the meals, and no hint of those little items of luxury that typified the tables of the gentry.

It was plain, from the preponderance of vegetables and fruit, that the bulk of provisions were supplied from Annabel's kitchen garden. Janet was inventive, but from his own experiences, Hal knew how little one could do with a few carrots and potatoes. Meat appeared once or twice a week, and Young Nat brought in dairy produce from the farm, where he worked in the smithy.

Preserves, pickles and juices were clearly home-made, and he had seen Janet baking bread. He was inclined to suspect that the ham which invariably made its appearance both at breakfast and luncheon had been smoked in the cottage chimney!

This was bad enough, and Hal longed for the freedom to make good the deficiencies of the larder beyond slipping in a brace of pigeons that he had purchased off a man who had undoubtedly been poaching the Abbey lands.

But Hal had also noted innumerable little jobs that needed to be done about the house. The boy Nat, whom he had observed chopping wood and handling the heavier work of an afternoon, had yet no eye for the little things. There was the loose casement in the big front room, and the one in the kitchen that would not open because of a broken latch. Several floorboards were up, and the kitchen stove smoked abominably, rendering the atmosphere hideous.

Hal had quietly soaped a couple of hinges when Annabel was out of the way, so that the parlour door and the back one that led to his own room no longer squeaked. And he had ventured an offer to Janet to fetch water from the pump on the green, which had been grudgingly accepted. But more he dared not attempt while Annabel held so strongly against him.

But nothing would serve to prevent him from seeking to acquaint himself with his little daughter! If he were to leave, he was horribly aware of the shortness of time he would have with her. And if he stayed—an idea with which he toyed rather too often—he already knew that Rebecca was the strongest incentive.

Yet it seemed that Annabel resented his interest

in his own child even more than she resented his coming here!

The little girl in his arms, however, began squirming to be put down. Hal set her on her feet, and saw that her attention had been caught by the imminent arrival of the maid.

"Dan-dan!" she cried, using her own corruption of Janet's name as she raced back towards the sturdy figure. Words bubbled off her tongue, as she began all over again the exhaustive tale of her adventure in the phaeton.

Hal turned to Annabel, and found her looking after the child. Deliberately, he entered upon a different subject.

"I met this fellow Tenison while I was out."

Annabel's gaze came back to his. "Our neighbour."

"But not your landlord, I believe."

"No, he is an absentee. Mr Maperton deals with the tenancies. He is a lawyer and lives in Abbot Giles."

"I hear from Tenison there is to be a fête on Saturday."

Annabel eyed him narrowly. "Yes, on the eighteenth. Lady Perceval holds one every year. What of it?"

God, but she was difficult! "I thought perhaps

Rebecca would like to attend it. Has she done so before?''

''Hardly. She was not yet two upon the last occasion.'' Her face became set. ''Besides, it is not my habit to hobnob with persons of the order of the Percevals. They are quite above my touch.''

Hal's lips tightened. ''You mean to imply that the blame for that must be set at my door.''

''I did not say so.''

''You have no need to say it, for it is obvious!''

Annabel with difficulty repressed a sharp retort. She looked away from him. ''Do you have a particular reason for wishing to attend the fête?''

''Beyond thinking of Rebecca's enjoyment? I don't doubt you will attribute to me some ulterior motive.''

Her eyes came back to his, suspicion in them. ''You said it, Hal, not me. But since you bring it up, do you have one?''

A rueful look came into his face, and he put up his fingers to smooth his moustache. ''You always were as sharp as needles! Very well. It struck me as an admirable opportunity to promote a general acceptance of my position here.''

''A cosy family outing?'' queried Annabel, her tone dry to conceal the leaden weight at her chest.

Hal grimaced. "A lie, I grant you, but a convenient one."

"For whom?"

He sighed wearily. "You will not let it alone for an instant, will you?"

Aware of the truth of this complaint, Annabel thrust down an urge to reply in kind. She turned towards the cottage.

"I will think it over."

Hal grasped her arm, swinging her round again to face him. "You hesitate only because I took Becky up in my phaeton—and without your permission. You are angry, yet you know it would be churlish to complain of it. So instead you taunt and carp at me! Is it to be ever thus between us, Annabel?"

She wrenched her arm away. "We are observed. If you care to display our disaffections in public, I do not!"

With which, she turned on her heel and swiftly re-entered the cottage before he could stop her again.

Hal stood fuming where she had left him, but his gaze involuntarily cast about in response to her words. To his annoyance, he saw that Weem, still holding the horses, was well within earshot. A couple of yokels, strolling past from the green, had paused to gawp. And the maid Janet, with the infant resting on her hip, had dallied on her way to the garden.

Cursing, Hal moved to his erstwhile batman. "I hope you have learned to be very deaf, Weem!"

"What's that you say, guv'nor?" responded the fellow, with a cheeky grin.

Hal threw his gaze heavenwards. "If I don't end by murdering you one of these days, it'll be in no wise your fault."

"Aye, if you don't strangle the missus first!"

"Damn your eyes, will you be quiet?"

"Close as an oyster, guv'nor," said his batman promptly, eyeing him with lively curiosity. He had reverted to his neat servant's garb of black breeches and a close jacket now that his identity was known here.

He glinted up at his master. "Speaking o' such, there's a deal o' talk roundabouts regarding the fellow what might have murdered this here mar-kiss."

"What fellow?" asked Hal, frowning, though it was not a question in which he had much interest.

"Solomon Burneck his name is. Though it'd better have been Solomon Surlyboots. A more determined miseryguts I hope I may never meet!

Between him and that witch of a laundrywoman—
old Aggie Binns, that is—there ain't nothing to
choose. If you ask me, they done in the markiss
between 'em. And if I'd 'a been him, with a son
like Solomon to me name, I'd 'a cut me own
throat long ago!''

It came as no surprise to Hal that his batman
was interesting himself in the affair. The fellow
could never keep his nose out of a mystery. He
owed to Weem the information that his own arrival had for the time being eclipsed the murder
in point of general discussion. Which was one reason why he had thought of using the coming fête
as a means of establishing the trio as a family in
the eyes of the locals.

But that scheme, he did not doubt, was blown.

The eighteenth dawned hot and clear. Annabel
had cherished a secret wish that it might rain, giving her a legitimate excuse to cry off from Lady
Perceval's fête. For her conscience had not allowed her to hold out against Hal, despite every
rebellious wish to do so.

There could be no denying the advantages of
showing herself abroad *en famille*, as it were. It
had more than once been borne in upon her, during her sojourn in the district these few years, that

Charlotte Filmer was not the only one to suspect the truth of her condition. To be able to confound the doubters by producing her "husband" resurrected from the grave was a satisfaction not lightly to be foregone.

Yet a sneaking desire to cry craven had pervaded her as the day approached. One needed a stout heart to carry through an outright falsehood—on every count!—and Annabel's heart was at this present very far from stout. She told herself that it was for Rebecca's sake that she made these sacrifices, as she sought through her meagre wardrobe for a suitable gown.

She chose one that she had fashioned herself a few months back. It was of the prevailing white muslin, quite plain. Worn with a neat straw bonnet and one of her old Norwich shawls—kept by from the days of her unshadowed life in London—it gave a perfect picture of the genteel young matron of respectable, if straitened, means.

To Hal, she looked distressingly indigent. The only fine thing about her costume was the embroidered shawl. And even he, relatively untutored in the matter of female dress, could tell that the gown was of poor cut and quality. Her financial circumstances no doubt prevented her from purchasing anything but the cheapest of dress-making services.

He had dignified the occasion with a frock-coat of blue broadcloth, with a toning waistcoat beneath, and breeches of grey linen, and he had set Weem to polish his boots to a shine and starch his neckcloth. There was nothing especially notable about his costume, but for the obvious quality of the materials and tailoring. But against Annabel's dowdy appearance, Hal felt he made a conspicuous figure of himself.

Nor was this the end of it. No sooner had they alighted from the phaeton, at a distance from the venue of the fête where a press of carriages prevented further progress, than Annabel was hailed by a friend. He could not be sure, but he thought it was one of the females who had been at the cottage on the day of his arrival but a week ago.

"Annabel, how delightfully that gown becomes you! Is it not the one you made up from that India muslin you purchased at Hammond's so cheaply?"

Dismay and guilt smote Hal. That Annabel had fashioned her gown herself had never entered his head. The suspicion crept into his mind that she was concealing from him the true nature of her situation. Worse was to come.

Mortified by her friend's unfortunate disclosure, Annabel was annoyed to feel herself flushing. "Yes, Jane." Attempting to change the subject, she added quickly, "I thought I might see you here. Are the other teachers also come?"

"Oh, yes, everyone. The girls would never forgive us if we did not bring them all to the fête. It is by way of a treat before they go home for the holidays. But, Annabel, I wonder if Hammond's might have more of that muslin this winter. I think I will bespeak another gown from you, if it should be so, even though you have already made one for me this year."

Aware of shock in Hal's eyes, Annabel made haste to deflect her friend with an introduction.

"I believe you have met Miss Emerson, Captain Lett?"

Hal bowed, but his attention was on the implication in the woman's last speech. Had Annabel been forced to take up dressmaking for others? And was that patterned oddity that sat so hideously upon the woman's admittedly graceful figure a specimen of her endeavours?

"I think we did not reach the stage of formal introduction," he said smoothly. "How do you do, Miss Emerson?"

Jane looked both pleased and flattered. Fearing

a tête-á-tête upon the subject of her gown, Annabel encouraged her friend to walk with them towards the ground where a multitude of bunting and ribbons upon poles protruding above the heads of the throng proclaimed the location of the event.

It appeared that all the world had come to the fair. It was crowded, and Hal lifted his daughter into his arms for fear of losing her. Annabel made no demur—indeed she was conscious of gratitude to be relieved of that duty, for the child was no longer a lightweight. He might as well make himself useful! And besides, she told herself fiercely, it was for Hal's purpose of displaying them as a family that she had consented to come.

Jane was soon seized upon by one of her pupils and dragged away. As Annabel strolled with Hal among the various booths, stopping here and there to watch a display of acrobatics or fire-eating which caught Rebecca's awed attention, she became acutely conscious that her new status had received a widespread report. She was obliged to present Hal over and again, as person after person came up to congratulate her on recovering her husband so unexpectedly. That she had never been on more than nodding acquaintance with the majority served only to reawaken her bitterness.

Hal received as much attention, and Annabel could not help a sneaking satisfaction in the reflection that he was obliged endlessly to repeat the story of his supposed escape from captivity.

Even Lady Perceval condescended to recognise her as they happened to pass within sight of the marked-off area given over to the patroness and her personal guests. The great lady gave Annabel both her hands.

"My dear Mrs Lett, allow me to offer you my deepest felicitations. And so this is Captain Lett? My dear ma'am, I heard that your fortunate husband is a dashing officer, and I see that this is indeed the case. But what an escape, sir!"

She carried on in this vein for several moments, until Annabel could have screamed. She conceived a reluctant admiration for Hal's sang-froid, for he rode through it all with ease, exuding charm. Only Hal had not been the despised poverty-stricken widow, who had now suddenly acquired a high degree of respectability.

Jane Emerson, seeking her out again at a moment when Hal had taken Becky off to see a puppet show, confirmed that this was indeed the case.

"What a triumph for you, Annabel! I cannot tell you the numbers of people who have chosen to count you into the fold this day. I myself heard

Lady Elizabeth Perceval and Mrs Rushford discussing the matter. Lady Elizabeth said she had always thought you a pretty-behaved young female, and Mrs Rushford declared that for her part, she had never believed there was the least reason to exclude you from her acquaintance.''

"I am obliged to her," said Annabel drily.

She had never received more than a nod from Mrs Rushford, despite the latter's own sadly reduced fortune and the scandal of her late husband's gaming debts. As for Lady Elizabeth Perceval, she could not remember to have been so much as noticed by her or her numerous offspring these three years.

"How thankful you must be for the workings of Providence," sighed Jane.

Annabel knew not what reply to make to this. It was clearly inappropriate to declare that she had been cursing Providence rather. It was galling to owe her sudden access of acceptability to the very man to whom she owed her fall! She could not but believe that the high sticklers who now deigned to notice her would sing a different tune did they know the truth. Yet a creeping apprehension could not but engage her with the thought of how her situation might alter were Hal to leave.

"Have you seen where they are performing the

puppet show, Jane?'' she asked. ''Captain Lett has taken Becky there, and I promised I would come after them.''

In fact, she had made no such promise, but it was the only excuse she could think of to get away from Jane's well-meaning but disturbing confidences. To her dismay, Jane offered to lead her to the place, and began to thread through the crowds.

Miss Emerson's progress, however, was interrupted a good many times by pupils from the Guarding Academy, who waylaid her, begging leave for some amusement, or wishing to drag her to this or that stall or exhibition. If it was not the bearded lady that she must see, it was the mermaid in a tank. One needed coins for a try at the ha'penny race track, another sought advice on which knot of ribbon offered for sale would best suit a particular gown. The cacophony was intense.

''Miss Emerson, may we not enter the dancing contest?''

''I think you should enter, Miss Emerson!''

''Miss Emerson, do you think Mrs Guarding will let us watch the ghost play? It is to be sharp at three o'clock.''

"Are we permitted to enter any of the races, Miss Emerson? I do so want to ride a donkey!"

While Jane dealt kindly but firmly with the motley requests, Annabel remained quietly at her side, confident that she was safe from the congratulations of well-wishers as long as she was around a school party.

She saw Hal at length, not in front of the little stage where the puppet show had taken place, but in a small arena where a number of farm animals were on display. Annabel caught sight of her daughter engrossed in patting the woolly coat of a sheep.

As soon as Hal noticed her, he went to Rebecca and bent to speak to her, pointing out Annabel. The little girl's face lit, and she came bounding up, one hand lost in Hal's large fingers. Annabel left her companion and went to meet Becky, picking her up for a hug.

"Have you had a lovely time?"

Becky proceeded to enumerate the delights she had enjoyed. In a moment, however, she seemed to remember something and asked to be put down. Then she stared up the lengthy distance into Hal's face.

"Where basket?"

Annabel saw him produce a covered basket

from behind his back. A small mew from within startled her, and the basket moved in a manner that was distinctly suspicious.

"Oh, no!"

"I am afraid so," said Hal apologetically, opening the lid. "I could not withstand her pleas."

Annabel looked at the black kitten with a good deal of misgiving. "Oh, Hal, for heaven's sake! What are we going to do with it?"

A tug at her petticoats demanded her attention. "Kitty, Mama."

"Yes, I know, darling. It's a lovely kitty, but—"

"Becca want kitty," piped up the child again, trying to reach the basket. "Papa! Me hold kitty."

The kitten faded into insignificance. A slow pulse began thumping in Annabel's chest. In a daze, she watched Hal hold the basket lower so that Rebecca could reach to the animal inside. *Papa.* She had called him Papa!

Hal felt the change in her. He handed the basket to his daughter, and straightened. Annabel was staring at him, her look compounded of reproach and another quality to which he could give no name. Her voice was low and accusing.

"You told her!"

* * *

Silence reigned in the phaeton. Rebecca's chatter had ceased. Tired out by the exertions of the day, she lay in Annabel's lap, lulled by the motion of the carriage into a light slumber. Only an occasional protesting mewl from the basket on the seat between them penetrated into the tense atmosphere.

Acutely conscious of the presence of Hal's man on the perch behind, Annabel was forced to bite her tongue on the tumbling volcano of her emotions. Hal had answered her accusation only with a look that signalled a violence of reaction that matched her own. He had then suggested that unless anyone required refreshment, they might with propriety leave the fête. Annabel could have eaten nothing at that moment, despite a gnawing hunger of which she was by now very much aware. If Rebecca had needed sustenance, it would have been a different matter. But she had partaken of several varieties of sweetmeat and ices through her sojourn at the fair, and so they had set off for the carriage without delay.

Prevented from engaging in a public display of temperament, and further disbarred by propriety from quarrelling either before a servant or her daughter, Annabel was obliged to bottle up her spleen. An unsatisfactory state of affairs that resulted in a redoubling of its power.

The phaeton was obliged to take a circuitous route through Steep Abbot to return to Steep Ride. As it entered that section of the road that ran across the lands of the late Marquis of Sywell, a diversion occurred.

Annabel was hailed by a passer-by, a creature in rusty black clothes, who stepped into the road and held up his hand to stop the carriage. Cursing, Hal pulled up.

"What in Hades—?"

"It is Solomon Burneck!" exclaimed Annabel in surprise. "I wonder what he wants with me."

Burneck shifted to Annabel's side of the phaeton and removed his hat. Misliking the look of the fellow—a disfavoured specimen with narrow-set eyes, thin lips and a slightly hooked nose— Hal glanced back at his batman.

"Get down, Weem, and be ready in case of trouble!"

Solomon, meanwhile, had begun upon an explanation of his peculiar conduct, but without the preliminary of greeting Annabel by name.

"Ye don't want to give notice to that Binns. As ye sow, so shall ye reap, as the good Lord said. It's poison she sows, Aggie, and she'll come by her deserts. Mark ye, she's not to be trusted.''

"Well, and what has it to do with me, Solomon?'' demanded Annabel forthrightly. "Are you warning me not to believe what she might say of your affairs?''

The thin lips sneered, and he shook his head. "I've no fear for my affairs. I know what I know, and one day I'll say it all. No one knew him like I did.''

Weem butted in. "Speaking of that markiss, are yer? If you take my advice, you'll spill all you know, and quick!''

Solomon did not deign to notice this interruption, but kept his eyes firmly on Annabel. "Ye be careful Aggie don't hear any more of ye than anyone else. Eyes in the back of her head, has Aggie. If you move, she'll squeak.''

"We don't need to listen to this!'' said Hal, preparing to give his horses the office to move on.

"Hop it, you!'' said Weem to Burneck.

"Wait!'' uttered Annabel tensely.

Did she owe it to Aggie then, that the world knew of Hal's return? Had the wretched woman already divined the dissension between herself and her bogus husband? Was that what the fellow meant? Solomon's still gaze remained fixed upon her. She nodded.

"She'll hear no secrets from me. Thank you, Solomon."

The man dipped his head as if in acquiescence, and then stepped back. Hal watched him replace his hat, and continue his walk without a backward glance. He signed to Weem to take his place behind and urged the horses onward.

"What was all that about?"

She threw him a brief look. "I should have thought it was obvious. Aggie Binns is indeed a poisonous creature." She turned to him, speaking with deliberation. "She lives within a stone's throw of my cottage. It is therefore necessary to be always circumspect."

Hal eyed her warily. There was irony in his voice. "I'll bear that in mind."

From behind him, Weem piped up. "True enough, guv'nor. I told yer so, didn't I? But yer don't want to go thinking that there Solomon ain't a shifty individual, missus, for he's as wily as they come."

"So I believe," Annabel agreed. "But it may be that he has been maligned. Perhaps he did not murder his master."

"I dunno," mused Weem. "He'd 'a been a

fool, to my way o' thinking. Always the first suspect they who is closest to the victim.''

Noting Annabel's astonishment, Hal felt compelled to offer an explanation. ''Weem is in some sort an intelligence agent, you must know.''

He then wished he had held his peace, for he received a flash from Annabel's green eyes, and her tone was cutting.

''I have had occasion to understand so, I believe.''

Clearly she had realised that he owed to Weem's offices his knowledge of her whereabouts. ''How did you guess?''

She did not answer him directly, but looked over her shoulder at the batman. ''Janet remembers you, Weem.''

He grinned. ''Aye, I reckoned to that. A right trimming she give me!''

''Undoubtedly deserved,'' commented Hal.

He thought he detected a slight relaxation in Annabel. If so, it vanished when Weem chose to take up the discussion again, addressing himself to Annabel.

''There's been things said, missus. I'd 'a told the guv'nor, only I didn't like to put me nose in where it ain't wanted.''

Annabel stiffened, but a desire to know the substance of any gossip that concerned her overcame her natural outrage. She half-turned in her seat, eyeing him suspiciously.

"What has been said? And by whom?"

Weem snorted. "Aggie Binns, missus. Who else?"

"Cut line, Weem, and speak out!"

"Aye, aye, guv'nor. See, missus, it's this way. That there Mrs Tenison what owns the big house over the way, she don't care who hears her talk seemingly. Nor she don't scruple to hand out how things ought to be to her way of thinking. She thinks guv'nor ought to up and take you away from here."

"Take me away?"

Annabel was unable to help a flying glance at Hal's face. She met his eyes briefly and found them fierce. Why? Had he thought of such a move? Or had it been his intention when he came—one that he had surely abandoned on receipt of her unwelcoming response to him! It had not occurred to her to consider the possibility of removing from Steep Ride.

Her heart pattered in her breast, for of all things in the world, she suddenly longed to be otherwhere.

"And if so be the guv'nor was to think to stay

in the district,'' went on Weem, apparently oblivious to the effect he had created, ''this Mrs Tenison says as how he ought to leave End Cottage, and instead hire that place up the road, what they call the Empty House.''

Annabel received this further intelligence with an increase of unsteadiness in her pulses. The Empty House, so styled by the locals because it had for years remained uninhabited, was much larger than her own poor dwelling. Almost as big as Datchet House, where Charlotte Filmer resided.

Without intent, her mind began to play with this possible rearrangement of her life. She might keep a proper parlour, and dine in a separate room from that which housed the detritus of day-to-day living. Rebecca could have her own playroom. And she might at last have space to spread her personal belongings in a bedchamber of adequate size.

Then she recalled that she would have to be indebted to Hal for all this. To possess it, she must indeed have reconciled herself to his remaining here. And that, despite the disordered leaping of her pulses, she knew she was by no means ready to do.

Their arrival at End Cottage was not much longer delayed, and Annabel wasted no time in putting her daughter to bed, leaving Hal to see to the new member of the household. It was the least he could do, she told him, having purchased the kitten against all common-sense.

Becky did not wake, and by the time Annabel had managed to change the child's garments for a nightgown and tuck her in, the effects of hunger were making themselves felt in no uncertain fashion. Something would have to be done.

Janet had been given the day off and was not due to return until morning. She had made a friend of the Yardley housekeeper at Jaffrey House, near to Abbot Giles, with whom she was no doubt enjoying a rare gossip while the gentry attended the fête. The Earl of Yardley's house being roomy, Janet was invariably invited to put up there on these occasions.

Annabel removed her shawl in her bedchamber, reflecting that Janet must have left a meal of sorts ready to be placed upon the table.

She could hear movement in the kitchen as she came down the stairs. To her astonishment, she discovered that the table was already laid with a cold collation. Sliced meats of ham and beef, a cheese, and a loaf of bread with several slices ready cut. Even as she turned, Hal came through the kitchen door bearing a tray which he laid down upon the table.

"I forgot the butter." He set out a dish, and proceeded to disgorge items from the tray. "I've made tea, but Weem bought wine at the fête." He lifted an uncorked squat bottle and sniffed the contents. "God knows what it's made of! Cowslips, probably, or something equally revolting. I told Weem to look out for a bottle or two, and this is what he comes up with! If I had not sent him off to the farm with the phaeton, I should have a deal to say to him."

Annabel watched in a bemused fashion as, like a conjuror, he produced cups and saucers, sugar and milk, and a couple of glasses. He had discarded his coat, displaying a waistcoat of light blue silk over his shirt. He looked, she was obliged to concede, excessively attractive.

Hal removed the tray, and set it aside. "I fed the kitten, by the by. Like Rebecca, it has succumbed to exhaustion."

She looked where he pointed, and saw the little black kitten curled up in a ball in one corner of the sofa. Then Hal was pulling out the chair at the head of the table which she usually occupied at meals.

"Come, Annabel. You must be both tired and hungry."

Automatically, she moved towards him, but paused before taking the seat. "You did all this?"

"Did you think I couldn't? I'm a soldier, Annabel. When you've bivouacked in as many different places as I have, you learn to fend for yourself. I can cook, too."

The note of mock pride in his voice drew a laugh from her. "Rabbit stew, I dare say."

"With turnips and onions, yes."

He set the chair for her as she sat down, and then went to take his own seat at the side. For several moments, he occupied himself with attending to her needs, and Annabel could not withstand a feeling of enjoyment at the unusual experience of having priority given to her comforts. And by a gentleman at that. It was a long time since she had partaken of a like indulgence.

She opted for tea, which did much to revive her flagging appetite, and for a time no thought of the wrongs she had stored up that day intervened in her mind to inhibit the satisfying of her first hunger.

But at length she sat back, and consented to drink a little of the wine which Hal pronounced to be tolerable.

"Unidentifiable from the taste, I may say, but it is pleasant enough."

He watched Annabel relax, her fingers curled around the glass. It was the first time since his arrival that there had been a semblance of normality in their dealings. The first time he was conscious of the faintest hope that there might be a chance for a future together.

Annabel had removed her bonnet and shawl, and her dark hair had loosened a little from its confining pins. He had not until now seen her without concealing headgear. It was just starting to darken outside, and light from the candles he had lit and placed on the table threw a glow upon her cheeks that was akin to the youthful bloom he had envisaged on the remembered image in his mind. At this moment, she looked to him so much like the Annabel he had loved that his chest tightened.

He dared not utter, for fear of breaking the spell. He did not want to reawaken the hating creature she had become.

As if she felt his regard, she turned her head and the green eyes met his gaze. They were the eyes of his vision. Eyes whose colour nearly resembled those of the black kitten behind them. Eyes of warmth and fire that he had carried with him through dirt, mire and battle, tormented by the undying passion they had inspired in his breast.

The years rolled away from him. Impulsively he reached out and his hand closed over her fingers where they rested on the white cloth.

''Marry me, Annabel.''

Chapter Five

Up leaped all the wellspring of emotion that was damped within Annabel's breast. Her throat ached and Hal's countenance became a blur.

"As easy as that?"

Hal was rising from his seat. Annabel felt herself dragged up from the chair. Next instant, she was locked close against his chest, and the thump of his heartbeat was mingling with her own. His face was near to hers. The face she had cursed a thousand times and hoped never to see again.

Fleeting and incongruous, came the realisation that Hal's features had changed. There were lines at the corners of his eyes and heavier ones underneath; grooves too, forming a path down the sides of his moustache, as of the marks of suffering. He was speaking, his voice low and passionate.

"It is there, Annabel! If you will let yourself feel it, it is still there. I thought it gone for ever, but it is not so. We can rekindle it, Annabel."

These words fell upon her ears like a douche of cold water. Rekindle *what*? The lust that had brought Rebecca into the world? He no longer had any love for her, that was plain. Had she not known it? She had deemed it dead, just as her own had died—and he had proved it to be so.

"Let me go."

She brought up her hands and made to push him away. Hal loosened his hold, but he did not release her. His eyes burned at her.

"You mean to deny it! You wrong me and yourself, Annabel."

"If I do, have I not cause?"

"I grant you that, but further wrongs will not mend what is past. Yet it can be mended."

Annabel pulled against his hold. "Let me go! I will not be coerced!"

Hal released her suddenly, and she almost fell away from him, catching at the table for support. He moved quickly, putting out a hand to assist her. Annabel slapped it away.

"Don't touch me!"

His ire rose, but he curbed it, shifting restlessly away the length of the table. He turned to confront her, and found her bowed down, her breath heavy. Grimness settled in his chest. How she was affected by him! Yet she refused to acknowledge it. She would not be coerced, she said. But he would coerce her! He would force her to the altar, if need be.

"We must be married, Annabel! For Rebecca's sake, if for no other."

She straightened up abruptly, a spark in her eye. "Oh, you have been busy there! Ingratiating yourself with her! Telling her who you are! Well, if you think to use my daughter as a lever, Captain Colton, you may think again!"

He flashed back. "For what do you take me? Do you think I would stoop to such petty blackmail? Ingratiate indeed!"

"I don't know what else you call it!"

He took a pace towards her. "By God, Annabel, if you were not such a cross-grained fool, you would know better! If I have tried to acquaint myself with the child, who shall blame me? What would you? She is my daughter too."

Annabel closed in, the bottled-up rage erupting out of her. "She is no more your daughter than the man in the moon!"

Hal could not withstand a sharp stab of apprehension. "What are you saying?"

"Oh, don't fear," she uttered scornfully. "You spawned her, Hal, but there it ends. You may seed the garden, but it is the gardener who tends the plants who matters most."

Relief swamped him. "Is that all? You have a fine turn for rhetoric, but your reasoning is false. I am her father, and I have rights."

Rights? Had he not abrogated those rights?

"You have no rights—not with her, nor with me. You dare to take that role upon yourself? You have not deserved it!"

"And whose fault is that?"

"*Yours*," she cried violently. "Yours, Hal, yours!"

Then she was closing with him, her fists clenched and beating at his silk-clad chest, punishing and pummelling as she had longed to do. Tears coursed down her cheeks, and she hardly noticed that Hal did nothing to stop her.

He stood and took the blows as he had not done that far-off day when the fury of her onslaught had ended in an act of illicit love. They did not hurt as much as he could have wished, for the sobs that wrenched from Annabel's throat tore him apart inside and made him glad of the minor torture. How little had he recognised the anguish she had endured! Three years of hell. And no matter her fa-

ther's hand in the sequel, it had been his mad act
of passion that began it all.

Annabel's violence rapidly spent itself, and she
all but staggered to the table, slumping into his
vacated chair and dropping her face into her hands.
Her shoulders heaved as she swallowed on the
racking sobs. Yet the first coherent thought in her
mind was despair at having lost control.

When she was able to raise her head at last, she
found Hal seated at the top of the table, regarding
her fixedly, one hand smoothing his moustache. He
held out a large square handkerchief.

Annabel took it and used it, reflecting that he
had matured a good deal. In the old days, he would
have fought her tooth and nail. She rolled the ruined handkerchief in a ball within her hands and
rested them on the tablecloth. She did not look at
him.

"I beg your pardon."

"Don't! Besides that I have long deserved it, I
think it has been building up for some days."

A faint smile crossed Annabel's lips and she
glanced fleetingly at him. "Years, perhaps."

There was silence for a space. Annabel felt benumbed, like the calm after a dam has burst when
one looks with scarce realisation at the damage.

Hal had asked her to marry him, she remembered. It had needed only that! Why had he said it?

As if he read her thought, he spoke again. "You were right, Annabel. It is not as easy as that."

Absently he massaged the short red hairs on his upper lip, his gaze filtering over the remains of their supper on the table. He had been deceived by an elusive memory into a foolish declaration. Too much lay between them. Had he been the one in denial? Trying to believe that his scheme—how unbelievably naïve it seemed to him now!—could cast a mantle of forgetfulness over the intervening years, as if they had never been. He had thought to take up where he had left off, with no thought for the damage that had been inflicted.

"What would you wish me to do, Annabel? I will go, if you prefer it. Do you want me to leave?"

Annabel felt a stirring at her breast. She looked at him, and the words that came out of her mouth were not at all what she intended.

"Do you want to leave, Hal?"

He could not answer for a moment. The green gaze was unreadable, as if a veil had fallen over her thoughts. Or was she merely spent? Without conscious decision, he opted for the truth.

"I don't know."

Her eyes dropped from his and fell upon her own hands. She found them clenched. With a fastidious gesture, she straightened them, setting aside the crumpled handkerchief. Curiously, Hal's words made her feel less hostile towards him. For the first time, perhaps, they were at one. She could have echoed him, for she no longer knew whether she wanted him to leave.

"If I hurt you by that, I am sorry." He sounded gruff.

Annabel absently reached for his discarded wineglass and sipped at the liquid it contained. Over the rim, she peeped at his face. He looked drawn, and he was frowning. She laid down the glass.

"It is the least hurtful thing you have said to me."

The wisp of a smile that accompanied her words was balm to Hal's sorely troubled conscience. He ventured to reopen the subject of Rebecca.

"There is much in favour of my remaining. From my viewpoint, that is." A mockery of a laugh escaped him. "I won't hazard an opinion upon yours."

"Better not," agreed Annabel drily, again sipping from his abandoned glass.

Hal felt oddly touched that she used it, as if they

were used to sharing. He tossed off the wine in the glass she had been using before and reached for the bottle, offering Annabel a refill.

"This will do, I thank you." She nursed the glass between her hands and looked at him. "Very well, enlighten me. What will you get out of staying here, Hal?"

He grimaced. "At the risk of enraging you again, I must say that I am loath to give up an acquaintance with Becky." No explosion greeted this disclosure and he was emboldened to continue. "I never thought it would be so, but the very sight of her—our hair so like there could be no mistaking the relationship!—was…" He laughed. "I don't know how to describe it. If there is such a thing as love at first sight, I think that must have been it!"

Warmth swept through Annabel. Just so had she felt, as the agonies of Rebecca's entry into the world were fading, when the doctor had first placed the wrapped bundle of tiny humanity into her arms.

"Yes, that precisely describes it."

"And when she called me Papa," pursued Hal, suddenly eager, "it seemed the most natural thing in the world."

He saw Annabel's features cloud, and remembered all at once her reaction at the fête. He leaned towards her.

"You blamed me for that, Annabel, but it wasn't my doing. To tell the truth, though it affected me, I doubt if the child knows the meaning of the word. She picked it up from the woman who sold us the kitten. She would keep looking to me, and suggesting to Becky that 'Papa' should buy it for her. Becky accepted the identification."

He recalled how the little features had lit up, looking at him with expectancy. "Papa buy kitty? Becca want kitty!" He had been as wax in her hands.

"You have not been at pains to give me a name for her use. She may not have heard me referred to in a way that she could understand—until that woman gave her something to grasp."

Annabel could well appreciate how it had happened. It made it no easier to bear, but the root of that was unworthy. She could not readily share Rebecca with Hal, and that was the plain truth of it.

"You need say nothing more. I see how it was."

"But you don't like it!"

She compressed her lips. "If you stay here, I shall be obliged to accustom myself to it, won't I?"

And so they were back to that. Hal took refuge in his wine. With a surge of emotion, he noted that Annabel was drumming her fingers on the table. So had she always done when her thoughts were troubled. Perhaps she had not greatly changed, after all. He plunged in.

"Aside from Becky—"

Annabel jumped. "I beg your pardon?"

"I was going to explain further what prompts me to remain here."

Her fingers stilled, but she did not look at him. "Do you think I don't know? You are driven by guilt! You see me in a situation which ill befits my status, and you blame yourself." She turned upon him a smouldering gaze. "Well, we have seen that it is not so. I never blamed you for what happened that night. No more than I blamed myself, at any rate. We were both grossly at fault."

"You may not have blamed me," said Hal harshly, "but for myself it is otherwise. Besides, you do blame me! That you made plain enough earlier this night. But let that pass. Suffice it that if I walked away then—by force of circumstance for I had no choice—I could not do so now. Not without having done what I might to alleviate your lot."

Annabel cringed inside. The last thing in the

world that she had ever wanted was his pity! "What had you in mind? An allowance? Or do you think, as Mrs Tenison evidently suggests, to set me up in the Empty House? Like a kept mistress!"

"Nothing could be more unlike!" retorted Hal. "If you want the truth, I have not thought beyond my horror at the exigencies of what you are obliged to endure. I could barely keep my tongue between my teeth when that female spoke today of your making her another gown. That you might be obliged to make your own gowns is bad enough. But if it is the case that you have found it necessary to set up as a seamstress, you may never guess at the depth of my remorse!"

It was, Annabel realised, exactly what she had wished for—that he should suffer the torment of knowing to what he had condemned her. Only it had not been his doing, she reminded herself. Had he had his way, she would have been safely married to him long before Rebecca was born. Instead of the satisfaction that was her due, she felt it incumbent upon her to mitigate his suffering.

"Lay that at my father's door rather. Or mine, if you wish. There was nothing to stop me from requesting that he increase the allowance he makes me."

"Nothing but pride." Hal dropped his head on

to one hand, kneading his brow a little. "You are too like him, Annabel, that is the trouble. We owe the situation we are presently in to your father's damned pride!"

Unexpectedly moved by his understanding of her predicament, Annabel was yet irritated by his readiness to prick at an old wound. She turned the subject.

"What would you do, were I ready to accept your aid?"

Hal shrugged, and his fingers dropped away. "Whatever you wish for, Annabel. I am the intruder here, and I know that my coming has disordered your life. It is useless for me to say that I did not mean it so, for all it is the truth."

To her own secret dismay, Annabel found herself displeased with this *carte blanche*. Yet why should she be surprised? Hal had made it clear enough that his emotions towards her had nothing to do with that old love. He would stay for Rebecca, and to make amends. Or he would go, making her financial compensation. Neither of which choices recommended themselves to her!

Almost without realising that she was playing for time, she rose from her chair. "Let us discuss it no further tonight. I am tired."

Hal stood up, putting out a hand. "One moment."

She paused, turning to look at him. Hal thought he detected strain in her features. Or was it merely the candlelight making them appear pale?

"Think of all the options, Annabel, if you think at all. I asked you earlier to marry me. I stand by it." He saw her about to speak and wafted a hand for her silence. "No, say nothing now. Give me an answer only when you have had time to think through the advantages. I can offer you a better life than this—both of you! Away from here. It was Mrs Tenison's notion—so Weem says—but it has its merits."

Common-sense decreed that he was right. But in this instance, Annabel could not be ruled by common-sense. She might go so far as to accept his aid, but marry him she could not! To live as man and wife, in a mockery of the desires they once had shared? No, a thousand times!

She shook her head, unable to let it pass. He must not for a single instant think that she could consent.

"Not that. Anything but that!"

With which she turned away from him, and went swiftly up the stairs, leaving Hal prey to a rise of bitter hurt.

* * *

The work for the Monday wash had increased since Hal's coming, although Annabel knew he was not aware that his discarded clothing had been added to the general load. It had not occurred to Young Nat, to whom Hal had confided his shirts, cravats and smalls, to do anything other than add them to the basket of laundry that Janet attended to each week.

The maid had grumbled, but Annabel had cut her short. "I will help you. It would embarrass me more, Janet, to be obliged to watch Captain Colton attending to his own washing than to endure what is, after all, but a trifling inconvenience."

"Trifling!" The maid had snorted. "I'll warrant you won't think so when it comes time to scrub it all! Why don't you send it to Aggie, ma'am?"

But that Annabel had refused to do. It would not have been politic to reject the services of Mrs Binns altogether, but Annabel had only ever sent the sheets to the local laundress. To put it bluntly, she could not afford Aggie's services in the general way. And nothing would induce her to ask Hal for money to pay for his own laundry to be done!

In one thing she had determined. She would not sue to him for financial help. No more had been said of his plans since the night of the fête.

Annabel had felt awkward in his presence, and had maintained a distant politeness.

She had seen him winning Becky over more and more—even now he had taken her for a morning walk—but had held her tongue upon the unnatural urge to come between them. He had been right when he said that the child had no understanding of his relationship to her. She used both "Hal" and "Papa" impartially, apparently under the impression that he went by both names. Guiltily aware that she ought to correct this, Annabel yet could not bring herself to make the necessary explanation. She excused herself with the reflection that there would be time enough to do so should she take up an option that permitted Hal to remain in his daughter's vicinity.

She was no nearer a decision now than she had been more than a week ago. To the world at large, they were a family. They ate together, and appeared together in public. No one could know— unless Young Nat had betrayed them, which Annabel would not believe to be possible—that Hal slept in an improvised bedchamber downstairs while she occupied the one above. And if by chance it was known, there might be speculation, but the true reason for it would not be visible.

She pegged a large shirt to the line, her fingers

lingering in its folds a moment or two longer than was necessary.

"You'd do better to stroke the real thing!"

Startled, Annabel's eyes flew to her maid's grim features. Janet was standing arms akimbo, eyeing her between the legs of a pair of undergarments. Annabel removed her fingers swiftly.

"What are you talking about?"

"You know what I mean, ma'am. When's it going to end, that's what I'd like to know?"

Annabel resisted an impulse to rebuke her for impertinence. Janet would only remind her of the occasions when she had been obliged to return the compliment. One could never reduce to their proper status of servants those who had guarded and scolded one as a child. Besides, without Janet, these last years would have been utterly unendurable. She had more than once given way to the need to sob out her heartache on that stern shoulder.

Defiantly, she lifted another shirt from the pile of damp clothing and began to attach it to the line. "It will end when I choose to make it end."

Janet sniffed. "If you'd any sense, you'd swallow down all them doubts and such, and be glad of your good fortune. If you ask me, you'd be a deal better off!"

Annabel eyed her with annoyance. "Would I, indeed? I suppose you would too! Well, you need not think I don't know why you've changed your tune."

"I ain't changed nothing," asserted the maid in her usual dour fashion. "It's you that has changed—only you're too much like the old gager to see it."

"If you mean that I resemble my father, you are telling me nothing I don't know. But if you are won over by a few minor adjustments to the house, I can only say that I am not."

Indignant, Janet paused with one of Rebecca's nightgowns in her hand. "The Captain's mended four floorboards, and got that dratted kitchen window to open and let all the smoke out. If you'd to cook in there in this summer heat, you'd soon know how 'minor' that was! And he promises to fix the stove an' all. If that boy weren't so lazy, he'd have done it himself long ago!"

There was justification for this complaint. Young Nat was useful, but inclined to skimp his tasks. He had been heard to grumble, so Janet had told her, because Hal had set him to work harder than he'd ever thought for—scouring and polishing all over the cottage. But since Hal did twice as much himself, in addition to chopping wood and fetching water as well as the various repairs he had accomplished, Annabel knew Nat's complaints had received short shrift from her maid.

Annabel had noted that Hal's activities had begun unobtrusively. Then, as she had made no demur, he had grown bolder, and already there were a number of tasks that he routinely undertook. While she acknowledged a sneaking gratitude for this unlooked-for assistance, Annabel was unable to disabuse her mind of the conviction that it was all part of his scheme to convince her that his presence was necessary to her comfort. The last thing Annabel wanted to concede.

And now here was Janet, urging her to encourage him! As she picked up one of her own shifts from the pile of washing, it was borne in on Annabel that her maid had intimated more than that. What had she said? *Stroke* him!

A sudden remembrance of that other time caused a surge of warmth to cascade into Annabel's bosom. Just as she recognised it, Annabel caught sight of Hal himself walking towards them from behind the cottage.

Embarrassment caused her to take refuge in attack. "Where is Becky? I hope you have not left her alone!"

"She is inside, playing with the kitten. I believe she is safe enough."

Annabel wanted at once to berate him, for she found his nonchalance profoundly irritating. Only she knew well that Rebecca would come to no harm, if left for a minute or two without supervision. If her attention was on Kitty this was doubly so. The unoriginal name had stuck, for when applied to for an appellation for her pet, she had reiterated only its generic name—and in no uncertain terms. "Kitty' it had therefore remained.

"I thought Kitty was here in the garden," Annabel said, for the kitten had certainly followed when she and Janet had emerged with the basket of laundry.

"One never notices cats leaving," Hal commented. "They are slippery creatures."

"Pesky little nuisance, if you ask me!"

"Oh, Janet, no. I know I was against it at the start, but Rebecca adores Kitty, and she is no trouble."

"No trouble to you," put in Hal. He grinned at the maid. "I dare say Janet would not mind so much if Kitty hadn't taken up her headquarters in the kitchen, for the purpose, if I am not much mistaken, of wheedling tidbits out of you."

To Annabel's annoyance, Janet visibly smirked.

"Gets under my feet, the dratted thing. And it's my belief, Captain, that it ain't a her but a him."

"You may be right."

He glanced at the washing-line as he spoke, and stared blankly at his own clothes. Annabel saw his features tighten, and stepped in, forestalling any comment.

"For heaven's sake, don't get upon your high ropes, Hal! There is no point in doing two washes a week, and Young Nat would not do your clothes half as well as we can."

He looked thunderous and his tone was clipped. "Had I an inkling that it would fall upon you, I'd have told Weem to do it."

"Why? You are doing enough about the house yourself. It is only fair exchange."

Hal held his peace on the protests bubbling inside him. To see Annabel working at a task fit for the likes of Aggie Binns could not but cut at him, driving in the guilt. Only now did he realise that she had again donned that working gown, its colour a faded rose. Like Janet, who was equally overworked, she wore an apron. And he could hardly speak his mind before the maid. He fell back upon what had brought him out here.

"When you are at leisure, Annabel, I would be glad of a word with you."

Annabel eyed him. "Upon what subject?"

He glanced at the maid, who had resumed the task of hanging up the washing. Janet sniffed.

"I can finish here, ma'am. It's plain enough the Captain wants to say his piece in private."

Hal could not forbear a smile. "You are nothing if not shrewd, Janet." He turned back to Annabel. "Besides, one of us should certainly check on Becky."

Annabel pegged out the shift she had been all the while holding in her hands, and followed him as he turned for the cottage. Rebecca was discovered to be happily occupied, having found a piece of string with which to inveigle the kitten into following her around the large room. Kitty's sudden pounces provoked the utmost delight, and Annabel allowed herself to be persuaded into the tiny parlour off to one side of the room near the front door.

"We will leave the door open, and you may hear that all is well."

His solicitude should have gratified her, but Annabel felt unaccountably irked by it as she took one of the two chairs. It was almost as if he had assumed a role as head of the family! And what in the world did he want to discuss?

Hal shoved open the small casement to let in much-needed air, and parked his large frame into the other chair. But his presence made the room look ridiculously small to Annabel. Really, if he was to remain with them, he could certainly not stay in this cottage. It was like a giant in a doll's house!

"I believe it is time that we looked at the business side of this arrangement," Hal began, without preliminary.

"What arrangement?"

Annabel noted his stiffening, and immediately regretted her tone. She sighed.

"I did not mean to snap."

"Habits are hard to break," he responded before he could stop himself. Then he threw up a hand. "No, forget I said that."

Annabel grimaced. "Under the circumstances, it is to be expected that we are both liable to be touchy."

Hal let out a laugh. "I think we should congratulate ourselves. It is more than a week since we last quarrelled."

"Since we last spoke, you might have said."

He eyed her warily. Was he to read anything into this softening in her manner? He felt as if a truce had been declared—shaky, but nevertheless an improvement on the previous tensions. Annabel had been meticulously polite, but withdrawn and stiff with him. For his part, he had felt as if he trod on eggshells. When she did not object to his doing things about the house, Hal had thrown himself into that work in a spirit of relief.

But the inevitable could not be postponed for ever. There was a limit to how far he could stand by and watch while Annabel lived under deprivations that he was in a position to rectify. He had made up his mind to talk to her, in any event, and the discovery that she had been attending to his personal laundry—with her own hands, devil take it!—had set the seal upon his patience.

He took his courage in his hands. ''Annabel, will you tell me upon what arrangements you are living here? I gather that your father pays you an allowance—which would appear to be woefully inadequate.''

Annabel instantly took this up. ''Inadequate for what? I am widow to a soldier, remember. It would scarcely be appropriate for me to be wallowing in the lap of luxury.''

''There is a difference between luxury and having the means to eke out the bare bones of a miserable existence.''

There was a good deal of acerbity in his voice, and Annabel found herself torn between gratification and a foolish desire to defend her father—who had indeed been ungenerous. She fought down the hot words that rose to her lips, and forced herself to speak with a calmness she was far from feeling.

"Well, and so what would you have me do?"

Hal made an effort to control his growing hostility. "Do you object to telling me just how you are placed?"

"Yes, I object strongly!"

He was silent, but Annabel read hurt in his eyes. She looked away. "You see what happens when we try to talk."

"It makes no matter. Rail at me if you wish. Only don't deprive me of the opportunity to do what I can to alleviate your situation. I owe you that, at the least."

It was upon the tip of her tongue to reject even this. It galled her beyond endurance to think that she might become beholden to him. Already Janet was in a way to believe that she ought to swallow her pride and take Hal back. And that only upon his activities in making the cottage more habitable. If Annabel were to accept pecuniary assistance from him, it would be hard indeed to stand out against his remaining.

But against that must be set the fact that Hal had some justification for his claims. He owed her *something*—if he could not give her love.

"Mr Maperton has charge of my allowance," she told him, regarding steadfastly the while her own hands aimlessly smoothing her apron. "He brings me a sum for my day-to-day needs each quarter, having extracted the amount of the rent for the cottage and other regular payments which he takes care of on my behalf. Indeed, he will be here on Friday."

The last day of July was looming, and perhaps it was as well, Annabel reflected, that Hal should be apprised of the situation before Mr Maperton arrived. She would not put it past him to make an untoward comment otherwise, should he be provoked into losing his temper.

"And the amount that Mr Howes allows you?"

Annabel looked at him then. It was degrading to be obliged to mention the sum, for she had long felt that it shamed both herself and her father. As a result, she threw the figure at him with defiance.

"It works out at a little over one hundred guineas, once the rent here has been paid."

Hal's brows snapped together. "A quarter?"

Annabel was so surprised by the question that she let out an involuntary laugh. "Are you mad? A year! Mr Maperton gives me in the region of twenty-five guineas. Oh, yes, and he pays Janet nine over and above that."

For several moments, Hal could not trust himself to speak. Rage burned in him, and he could readily have held a gun to the head of the man he had once thought to take for his father-in-law. Howes put a roof over his daughter's head, and paid for the services of a maid. Beyond that, he expected her—with a child dependent upon her!—to manage on little more than one would pay a governess. Less in fact—for the governess would live at the expense of her employer.

Annabel must feed and clothe all three of them, not to mention cook and clean and warm the house. Iniquitous! Had the fellow no shame? Had he no heart? Or was his vengeance so extreme that he could visit it upon his daughter, as well as upon the lover who would have rescued her from the consequences of his actions?

He had no idea how his face gave him away. Annabel was touched. She had grown used in these past years to scrimp and scrape to make ends meet. She had all but forgotten that there had been a time when she had spent upon a single gown an amount that now served her for several weeks. But Hal had last seen her wearing one of those same expensive gowns.

"It shocks you, I see that."

Hal erupted out of the chair. "It disgusts me rather!"

He moved to the window, and clenched one hand on the sill. He spoke with his back to the room, rigidly controlled.

"I never dreamed that Howes could serve you so. That you were purse-pinched has been evident from the first, but I had not supposed for one moment that things were as bad as that."

Annabel said nothing. To see him so genuinely upset on her behalf—without taking more blame to himself for once!—could not but warm her heart. He turned his head, and she was startled to see tears in his eyes.

"You must hate me indeed. And for the life of me, I cannot blame you."

His gaze returned to the view of the village green which stood a few hundred yards beyond the parlour window. He could not say what he felt— that this altered everything. Had he not said at the outset to Ned that his honour was at stake? Only he had not known then how truly he had spoken. It was no longer merely a question of making amends. He could not live away from here with the slightest peace of mind, knowing that his child, and the woman who bore her, were condemned to a life of penury.

"I wish you will not make too much of it, Hal."

He turned sharply. Annabel had risen, and was standing in the parlour doorway, ready to leave the room. He started forward.

"Don't go!"

She waited, more moved than she had thought by the look in his face. "What is it? Do you wish to tell me that my father has wronged me? I know it already."

Hal reached her, and took her by the shoulders. "Why, Annabel? Why did he do this to you?"

She shifted uncomfortably. "I disappointed him. I believe he wanted to punish me for that. I did not know then that he had also punished you."

He released her, and stepped back. "Is that what you think? I don't believe you know him, Annabel."

"Better than you at least."

He looked as if he was about to say more, but to her puzzlement he shifted away again, moving to the slim mantel and leaning one elbow upon it.

"You should have lived a very different kind of life," he said heavily. "That you did not must be laid to my account."

Annabel threw her eyes heavenwards. "I thought it would not be long before you took to blaming yourself again."

"How can I help it, when I see you performing menial tasks? And it is now apparent why you have been driven to take up tailoring. I can never sufficiently regret my part!"

To his surprise, Annabel crossed the small room. She was before him all at once, and he felt his hand clasped between both of hers. For the first time in all their dealings, a smile of real warmth softened her features.

"Hal, I may have been bitter towards you, and I may rail at you again. Yes, my life is hard, and I could have shared your regret for what happened that night, but for one circumstance. I would not otherwise have had Rebecca. How could I ever regret her coming into my life?"

His heart twisted. His hand turned within her clasp and seized her fingers. Then one arm was about her shoulders, and he was drawing her closer. Huskily he breathed her name.

"Annabel."

Her face changed. Alarm was in the green eyes. Then Annabel was pushing him away.

"No! I am not so easily to be caught this time, Captain Colton!"

Next moment, she was gone from the room.

Chapter Six

Annabel tried hard to be glad for Charlotte Filmer's sake. But it was difficult when her own situation was so very uncertain.

Her neighbour and friend had hurried over with the extraordinary tidings in a state of great excitement. Even the flurry of rain in the morning that had left the ground damp had not deterred her. She looked as if she could scarce sit still in the sofa she was occupying, and it was evident that she had barely been able to contain herself to ask after Rebecca, who was taking a nap as she did now and then in the afternoon.

It was indeed occasion for excitement. "Athene is betrothed?" Annabel refrained from expressing her astonishment. "That is happy news for you, Charlotte. Who is the man?"

"Nicholas Cameron," announced Mrs Filmer proudly, twitching her petticoats. "A gentleman, and a Scot. His cousin is the Earl of Kinloch."

The recital of Mr Cameron's manifold attractions, together with the proposed plans of the engaged couple, took some time. It appeared that Athene was coming home, bringing her betrothed, before returning to London for the wedding. At the end, Annabel, having responded suitably, was moved to indulge in cynicism.

"A rare end to Athene's task of chaperoning the Tenison girl. How Mrs Tenison will be set down!"

Charlotte tutted. "Now, Annabel, you know I was excessively grateful to Mrs Tenison for taking Athene to London." Her pretty features grew a pink. "But I must confess that it does give one a fillip to discover that one's despised position in the neighbourhood is to be reversed all at once."

Annabel repressed an inclination to make a caustic reply, but could not forbear a flying glance at Hal, who had pulled round one of the dining-seats for himself, since Annabel had taken the armchair.

"It is certainly something of a change."

Her voice was taut, Hal noted. It was nothing new. She had been distinctly edgy these two days. Perhaps fortunately, business had taken him out for most of yesterday, and this woman's arrival this morning fortuitously intervened to keep at bay any possibility of a tête-à-tête. He had not joined in the conversation, beyond the requisite politenesses. But this must be nipped in the bud. It would not do for the visitor to divine the dissension between them. He spoke bluntly.

"Mrs Lett refers to her own recent experience."

Annabel threw him a look that spoke volumes, but Charlotte Filmer had already picked up on it. She gave a breathless little laugh.

"Dear me, I had forgotten. I had no intention of reminding you of it, Annabel. Have you been much displeased by the talk?"

"It has not come much in my notice since the fête, I am happy to say. And Mrs Tenison has thankfully refrained from descending upon me."

Determined to create an impression of harmony, Hal rose and came across to her chair, perching on the arm. "But that, my love, is because I am only an army captain. I imagine Mrs Filmer's daughter, with an Earl attached to her betrothed—" bending his most charming smile upon the lady opposite "—is unlikely to escape the attentions of the great lady of the district."

Annabel sat rigid, so disturbed by his nearness that she could not think straight, let alone formulate anything to say. What in the world he thought he was doing by this, she could not imagine! Thankfully, she saw that Charlotte's attention was upon what he had said. The visitor was a trifle indignant.

"If anyone is the great lady here, Captain Lett, it is certainly not Mrs Tenison. She may put on airs, but you will see her kow-tow gracefully to Lady Perceval, I assure you."

Somehow Hal's arm had snaked around Annabel's shoulders. She stiffened, shifting with discomfort. Was this a charade for the benefit of her friend?

Hal was laughing—with a nonchalance that made her want to hit him.

"I should be astonished to see her kow-tow to anyone, Mrs Filmer. I like her husband, however. A sensible fellow is George Tenison. He has been most helpful to me."

Annabel turned abruptly, and his arm fell away. "You have said nothing of this. How has he been helpful?"

To her annoyance, he looked bland. "Did I not tell you, my sweet? That was remiss of me. Tenison has been so good as to present me to some of the local gentlemen. And he is acquainted with your fellow Maperton, whom I was anxious to meet—as you know."

She was obliged to exercise great self-restraint to refrain from bursting out. But Hal was turning to give polite attention to Charlotte.

''Maperton is an excellent man!'' she was saying. ''We are so fortunate to have him rather than Sywell for our landlord. Or rather, his agent. Not, of course, that we would have Sywell any longer. Dear me, I wonder what will become of his property?''

Speculation about Sywell's heir had been strong immediately after his murder, but at this present Annabel had scant interest in the matter. With Mrs Filmer, however, it was otherwise.

''Oh, that reminds me. In her letter Athene also gave me to understand something very odd indeed. I would not mention it to anyone but you, Annabel. And I am sure Captain Lett can be trusted.''

Hal reassured her, and contrived at the same time to lean back upon the arm of the chair in a manner that made it impossible for Annabel to do other than rest against his shoulder. She was hardly able to give attention to what Charlotte was saying.

''Athene says that she has it from someone who *must* know—you may readily guess who, though I mention no names!—that Solomon Burneck was indeed the Marquis's by-blow.''

Annabel was in no condition to guess anything

at all, let alone the mysterious identity thus hinted at. Fortunately, Mrs Filmer had not completed her disclosures.

''And you know how we all wonder if Solomon killed him. Well, in London it is said that Yardley is more strongly suspected.''

Hal entered the lists at this. ''Ah, that is not Weem's opinion, though I believe the Runner who has been sent down to investigate the affair has his reasons for believing the Earl of Yardley to have been involved.''

''What in the world do you know about it, Hal?'' asked Annabel, surprised into forgetting his disgraceful conduct.

''Weem—'' with a quick smile to Charlotte ''—my batman, you must know, has been interesting himself in the affair. It is his considered opinion that Burneck did the deed, even though the fellow can prove he was not at the Abbey on the fateful night, and Yardley was.''

''Oh, this is ridiculous!'' Driven by the discomfort of Hal's closeness, Annabel took the opportunity to pull away and sit straighter in her chair. ''No one really knows anything. And I don't see why we should be discussing that wretched man's murder when we ought rather to be talking of Charlotte's excellent news.''

She stood up as she spoke, and crossed to the sofa, putting an arm about her friend and giving her a hug.

"It is wonderful for you, Charlotte, and I hope very much that Athene will be delightfully happy. Will you remove from here when they are married?"

Mrs Filmer looked flustered. "I hardly know. I should suppose not. I could not wish myself upon them. I mean, a young couple need privacy." She patted Annabel's hand briefly. "It is why, I suspect, everyone has been leaving you to yourselves in these early days."

"You may have done so for that reason, Charlotte," returned Annabel drily. "I hardly think those further afield are motivated by a like consideration. But I should be surprised if Athene does not wish for you."

"Well, she may, but I shall not go to her!" declared Mrs Filmer, uncharacteristically firm. "Though I must confess the place has become odious to me since all this dreadful business over Sywell so that I should be only too happy to go— if it were not to depend upon Athene. What about you, Annabel? Have you thought of removing from here, Captain Lett?"

Hal glanced briefly at Annabel's face. The green

eyes all but dared him to pursue the subject. He turned to the visitor.

"It is one of the options under discussion. However, we are not yet decided just what we are going to do."

"But you have sold out? I think I heard so from Mr Hartwell."

With shock, Annabel heard him admit it. How long had the vicar known? For how long had it been known to the neighbourhood, so that any attempt at putting it about that Captain Lett had been recalled to his regiment must be received with disbelief? If he were to leave, what possible excuse could she formulate, without it being readily understood that they had separated? She quickly realised that there was none. She was trapped.

How she kept from attacking him while Charlotte remained with them, Annabel did not know. But no sooner had the front door closed behind the visitor than she let fly.

"You knew this! You knew it at the outset! How could you allow me to think that I had a choice in the matter?"

"Keep your voice down! You will wake Becky."

Annabel stormed to the parlour, from where the sound could not penetrate so easily. She had equally forgotten the ears of Janet, cooking in the kitchen next door. Taking up a stance in the middle of the little room, she waited for Hal to appear, and watched him shut the door with care.

"You have deceived me!" she accused, low and vibrant. "And as for that pretence of affection—!" Words failed her, and she all but ground her teeth.

"Do you wish people to know the true situation?" Hal went to the window and closed it. "There. Now you may screech at me to your heart's content, and none the wiser."

Curiously, this permission had the effect of damping Annabel's fury a little. Yet she glared at him.

"Will you give me an answer?"

Hal shrugged, tugging at his moustache. "If I give you the truth, you will only suppose that I am lying."

"Try me." She gripped her fingers tightly together. "I need *something*."

His tone was mocking. "What you mean is that you need a reason to feed your anger. I will not give it to you. Suffice it that my actions are geared to one end—that of shouldering my responsibilities. If you wish to argue with that, then so be it."

Annabel turned her back on him, wishing for

space in which to rage up and down. She longed to get out where she might pace out the restless agitation of her spirits. But to do so would expose her situation to any prying eye that cared to pass. She had enough pride yet, she hoped, to refrain from publicising her discontent.

"Annabel."

There was a plea in his voice, and Annabel lifted her hands to shut it from her ears. She did not want to hear him. She did not want to be seduced by that persuasive tone—so reminiscent of the days long gone when he had but to speak, and she would melt into his arms.

"God help me, I am *caged*."

She sounded desolate, and Hal's chest went hollow. Was it the truth? Was she yet so much against him? Impulsively, he offered her all the palliative he could call to mind.

"That people know I have sold out need not be a bar to my going, if that is what you fear." Not that he had any intention of going, but he must find a way to alleviate the evident stress she felt at the thought of his continued presence. "There are other solutions, besides my being recalled to duty."

She did not turn, and her hands, which had

dropped from her ears to clench upon her own arms, did not shift.

"For all the world knows," he pursued, "I may be in need of employment. I could engage upon business that would take me away for the better part of the year. I could have family affairs to attend to." He paused in desperate thought, and was hit by a novel notion. It was with enthusiasm now that he resumed. "Better still, I might go abroad in pursuit of furthering our fortunes. To the West Indies or the Americas. It would not be unreasonable to leave you both safe here while I spied out the possibilities."

He saw that Annabel's shoulders were relaxing a little, and her hands dropped from about herself. He spoke again, developing his theme, even as his feelings pressed for utterance. entirely removed from what he said.

"And if you wish for it, any possible return could be utterly quashed. 'Captain Lett' could be taken off—by a mysterious fever perhaps. Or a colic. Lost in a hurricane. Shot in a riot. Yes, I fancy there will be no difficulty in being rid of me for ever. There is no end to the ways you might be widowed again!"

Annabel turned, and showed him a countenance given over to laughter, albeit reluctant. "I wish you will not be so absurd! How could I wish for your death?''

Hal grinned. ''Ah, but I would not be dead, and only you would know it.''

She drew a sighing breath. ''Hal, that is not a solution.''

He grimaced, treading closer. ''I know, but I don't want you to feel yourself to be trapped.''

''But I am trapped! If I send you away, I will be guilty of as foolish a pride as my father. There is no question but that your presence here must change our situation for the better. I could condemn myself to continue in the same way, but I can't do that to Rebecca.''

''Then at last we are of one mind!''

Annabel looked him boldly in the face. ''Yes, very well. But you need not suppose that my agreement in this extends to allowing the sort of familiarities you dared to take in Charlotte's presence.''

Anger lit in Hal's breast. ''As far as the world is concerned, I am entitled to take more intimate liberties! You must accustom yourself, if you do not wish the world to know that we sleep apart.''

A hot flush rose up into Annabel's cheeks, and her temper flared. ''Let them know it! I will not have my dignity abused merely for the sake of appearances.''

Hal could not contain a surge of bitter hurt. "You were not concerned with your dignity three years ago!"

Annabel struck him.

His cheek smarting, Hal seized her wrist, and twisted her arm behind her back, holding her chest to chest. Her other arm became trapped between them. She panted up at him, defiant.

"You dare to taunt me!"

"If you again hit out, wildcat, I swear I will use you just as if I were your husband!"

Annabel jerked, but he held her fast. "Spare your threats! I will fight you with every breath left in my body, and you know it."

For answer, Hal bent his head and fastened his lips to hers. Sheer instinct made him do it. Within seconds he was caught up in a dizzying sensation of *déjà vu*. The warmth of her mouth, as her lips slipped open below his own; the feel of her body in his arms; and the flare and flame of his loins. All just as he remembered it.

For several instants, Annabel held out against the force of heat engendered by his violent caress. But the flooding fire would not be denied. Her breath shortened, and without will she melted into Hal's embrace.

But the madness was of short duration. As he

came up for air, his grip relaxed. Annabel shot into realisation, and pushed frantically away from him, sputtering protests.

"Is there—to be—no end? What are you t-trying to do to me? No, don't touch me!"

This because Hal, dazed with the shock of it, had reached out for her again. Then he, too, recollected the present. Hastily, he stepped back, confusion in his features. Seeing it, Annabel experienced a resurgence of that dread feeling that had overtaken her on that first day. For the life of her, she could not keep her tongue.

"You must be insane! When you saw me first, you were shocked. I repelled you. Don't try to deny it!"

Hal, bemused and foggy still, blundered into agreement. "I don't deny it. You looked so different—you still do. Only I have grown used to you, I suppose. Underneath you are the same, Annabel."

Outrage churned inside her. Oh, had she not known it? Why did he not say outright that her appearance was repulsive to him? It was what he meant! Grown used to her? She ought to thank him!

"Pray don't imagine I have any desire that you should repeat yourself," she said acidly. "I may have to tolerate your presence in the house, but I will be obliged if you will in future keep your distance!''

She was *en route* to the door as she spoke. Hal made no attempt to stop her, merely stepping aside with an ironic little bow.

''Have no fear! I have no intention of inflicting my attentions where they are clearly unwelcome.''

Annabel threw him a scorching glance over her shoulder, and left the parlour as quickly as her shaking legs would allow.

Mr Maperton was a dapper little man, neatly dressed in a countrified way in a sober frock-coat suited to his calling, and black cord breeches.

''Ah now, yes. It is here somewhere. Now, let me see,'' he said primly, searching in his bag in the scattered manner habitual to him. ''I know I put it—ah, now, there you are, you flighty creature!''

Triumphant, he extracted a thin sheaf of papers, neatly tied up with red ribbon. Laying it on the table, he then sought in several pockets for his spectacles, tutting fussily the while.

Annabel strove for patience. It was a commodity in short supply these days. She had found herself snapping at Rebecca, to her shame. A well-deserved rebuke from Janet had caused her to apologise, and Becky had forgiven her upon receipt of a hug and a kiss. As for Captain Colton, she made no attempt at patience! Indeed, she had scarcely addressed him at all beyond the strict essentials.

That he had remained indoors this Friday morning, on purpose to meet the lawyer, she endured with ill-concealed annoyance. He might well have accompanied Rebecca into the garden, saving Janet the duty of minding her while she played with her pet. But, no. For reasons known only to himself, he chose to stay, despite her one short comment that her meeting with the lawyer had nothing to do with him. Hal had regarded her in a manner infuriatingly enigmatic, and folded his arms. Short of brute force, there had seemed to be no way of getting him out!

The lawyer found his spectacles, placed them on his nose, and picked up the packet of documents. ''Now, Mrs Lett, these are the papers concerning this establishment which you had consigned to my care.''

Annabel frowned. ''Very well, but why have you brought them?''

Mr Maperton wagged a finger. ''Ah, Mrs Lett, there's the nub. Happy as I am to have been of service to you, it gives me greater pleasure to be able to relinquish my duties into the capable hands of your husband.''

He gestured as he spoke towards the end of the table where Hal was standing behind her. Annabel turned to glance at him in puzzlement. He was regarding her gravely, but he said nothing. She turned back to Maperton.

''But who has asked you to relinquish them?''

''Why, Captain Lett, naturally, ma'am,'' said the lawyer, surprised. He laid down the papers again. ''He came to see me, and we settled it all right and tight between us. Last Tuesday, I believe, was it not, sir?''

''Quite right, Mr Maperton.''

Hal shifted away from the table and into the room, the better to see Annabel's face. He had expected her fury, and had meant to have told her on Wednesday—before, that was, they had quarrelled again. She was staring at him, but she looked to be more shocked than angry.

Annabel was in fact dumbfounded. Hal had assumed control of her affairs? And without so much as telling her! Never mind *asking*. It was plain now why he had remained for this interview. For an endless moment, she could only gaze at him numbly, scarcely hearing what the lawyer was saying to her.

"I hope I may be permitted to congratulate you, Mrs Lett, upon this joyous occasion. If you will not mind my saying so, your situation has grieved me very much. I must say that I am thankful, for your sake, that Captain Lett is in a position to remedy matters."

Vaguely Annabel took in the content of this speech. More or less at random, she tried to answer.

"Yes—thank you. I mean, you are very good. I do not know precisely what..." She faded out, looking instinctively to Hal, as if she supposed he must understand her confusion.

Nor did he fail her. "Mr Maperton has been very helpful, my dear. Between us, I think we have hit upon a few workable improvements."

"Indeed, yes," agreed the lawyer eagerly, removing his spectacles and putting them first in one pocket, and then another as he spoke. "An excellent scheme to remove to the larger dwelling."

"Larger dwelling?"

"He means the Empty House. I have taken the lease for a month to start with. It needs a great deal doing to it to make it habitable, I'm afraid, but it has stabling for my horses, which can be put to immediate use, and will be much more convenient than the farm. And I will put Weem to work to see if the place may readily be set to rights.''

''Ah, but any repairs must be undertaken by my principal, Captain Lett.''

''Yes, so you said. But since he is an absentee landlord, and it may take you time to contact him, I believe I must begin in my own fashion. Be sure I shall bill your principal if I should be compelled to make any serious outlay.''

Annabel listened with only half her attention as the two men argued the matter back and forth. Mr Maperton evidently felt that the owner should agree to the repairs before any costs were defrayed, but Hal took it upon himself to make good any losses incurred.

Took it upon himself! He had taken a great deal upon himself—and without reference to her. Oh, she cared nothing for his leasing the Empty House for his own use. But that he could take her affairs in hand behind her back was beyond anything! And just how had he done so? *What* had he done? She interrupted the discussion without ceremony.

''Mr Maperton!''

He turned to her and bowed. ''Mrs Lett?''

''I beg your pardon, but these arrangements have been made without my knowledge.''

She saw his surprise, and noted Hal's chagrin,

but she did not care. She would not be coerced!
Had she not told him so repeatedly?

"What I wish to know," she continued in a determined way, "is just what Captain—" She
choked off the name Colton, and resumed. "What
exactly has Captain Lett done as regards my own
affairs?"

Hal came to her side. His tone was clipped.
"You have no need to question Maperton. I will
tell you everything."

"Just as you told me you had been to see him?"

The lawyer began to look uncomfortable, but
Annabel was beyond considering his feelings. She
turned to him, but Hal intervened again before she
could speak.

"You may as well know, Mr Maperton, that my
return has not been as easy as people might suppose. I have no doubt I can rely on your discre-
tion?"

Annabel stood rigid as the lawyer assured him
that no word of the conversation should pass his
lips.

"Very well, then. Be so good as to explain to
my wife just what arrangements were agreed."

The lawyer was hunting frantically for his spectacles, clearly having forgotten in which pocket
they had finished up.

"Ahem. Your—er—husband has taken a strict examination of the terms under which you have been paid, Mrs Lett. I have shown him all the relevant documents."

Wrath burned in Annabel's breast. What? Had he had the temerity to look at Papa's letters to Maperton? Was he now familiar with all that had passed between them? If so, he knew more than she did herself!

But the lawyer had not finished. "The rents, as you know, have been paid out of the sum entrusted to me by Mr Howes. The Captain has engaged to pay them himself, so that the residue can be given into your hands entirely. And he has given me notice that his bankers will submit a further sum of five and thirty guineas a quarter for your use."

Annabel blinked at him. "Five and thirty guineas! Every quarter?"

Mr Maperton rummaged in his bag, bringing out the familiar leather purse from which he usually paid her allowance. He solemnly counted out several large bills and a quantity of guineas on to the table.

"If you wish for more or less of it in coin or bills, you have only to tell me."

The burgeoning fury was ludicrously dashed. Dazed, she stared at the coins and bills. The sum seemed a fortune. And Hal had done this! She recalled something the lawyer had said.

"But his bankers cannot have sent this money already."

"Captain Lett wished to put in the change immediately," explained Maperton. "He happened to have sufficient funds about him to make good the deficiency." He coughed, eyeing Annabel doubtfully. "I did venture to suggest that the Captain might deal directly with any payments, but he inferred that it was possible he might be from home, and that it was easier for you to continue to pay your way as you had been used to do."

Annabel could not utter a word. She had readied herself for battle, and had been defeated without a shot fired. What could she say? Before she could gather her wits, Hal was once more addressing the lawyer.

"I think it would be as well, Mr Maperton, if you continued to hold the legal documents pertaining to the lease." Moving to the table, he picked up the sheaf of papers and placed it in the lawyer's hands. "My movements are uncertain, and Mrs Lett may more readily rely upon your good offices. I should not wish her to have to hunt the house for these documents should I be absent."

The lawyer soon departed, having refused a

glass of wine on the score of having a number of other tenants to visit before his return to Abbot Giles. Annabel bid him goodbye without knowing what she said, and watched Hal escort him to the front door of the cottage.

Inconsequently, her mind ran on the offer of wine. Was it the cowslip wine—or whatever it might have been that his batman had obtained at the fête—that Hal had intended he should drink? Or had he set in a store of bottles unbeknownst to her? Clearly she knew little of what he would be at!

When Hal returned, he stood just within the confines of the family room, his eyes upon her, his fingers playing an uneasy dance upon his moustache. Annabel met his glance.

"You might have told me—asked me, even."

He shrugged. "If I had, I knew you would refuse it."

"Aid on such a scale? Of course I would have done so!"

"It is little enough."

Once he had ascertained what his new estate could stand, he had the intention of increasing the amount. That was, if a better solution could not be attained. But there was no speaking of that!

Annabel shifted to the sofa and sat down, drum-

ming her fingers on the arm. Hal did not move
from where he stood, warily watching her. She had
put on the sprigged gown in which he had first seen
her here, presumably for the lawyer's visit. It had
seemed dowdy to him then. But against the rest of
her wardrobe, it was clearly one of her best. Well,
she might do better for herself now—if she did not
repudiate his assistance.

Her gaze came up again, and Hal saw with pain
that there was real trouble there.

"Oh, Hal, what a position you have put me
into."

He stepped a pace into the room. "How so?"

Annabel found it difficult to put into words. She
did not fully understand herself the sense of dis-
satisfaction that beset her. While he was only an
intruder—his word, not her own!—she might berate him with impunity. But to be thus beholden.
Oh, it was intolerable!

Uncannily, Hal appeared to read her mind. "Are
you thinking that you are now in debt to me?" A
harsh note entered his voice. "You have nothing
for which to reproach yourself. You may continue
to regard me in whatever light you choose. I owe
you this, Annabel. I have told you so often enough.
And whatever there is between us, we are agreed,
are we not, that Rebecca's needs come first?"

She could not deny it. Yet how easy it was for him to talk of the light in which she might regard him. How was she to avoid feeling indebted? And feeling thus, she could not but be inhibited in her dealings with him.

Her eye caught the guineas on the table, which she had not touched. Despite her misgivings, the relief of the enlargement to her funds was intense. She had at her disposal more than twice what she had before. She might never set another stitch! The little box in which she kept her money—in a secret cache in her bedroom of which not even Janet knew the location—had never contained a like amount.

Her throat ached suddenly. She looked up, and Hal's features splintered in the mist that rose before her eyes.

"Thank you."

Abruptly, he strode to the table. "Don't thank me. I can bear anything but that." He scooped up the bills and coins. "Where do you keep your money?"

Without a word, Annabel rose up and climbed the stairs. Reaching her bedchamber, she sought under the loose floorboard for the little wooden box. She rose with it in her hands, and almost bumped into Hal as she turned.

She gasped a little. "You gave me a fright!"

"I beg your pardon."

He said it absently, for he was looking over the cluttered room. It was situated immediately above the larger of the downstairs rooms, but it looked a good deal smaller. There was a four-poster which, though itself no more than four feet in width, more or less dwarfed the rest of the space. A chest and a press filled the other wall, and a basin and ewer stood on a wash-stand in a corner. Aside from the furnishings, all of which were of the plainest wood, a quantity of odds and ends of haberdashery had been piled to one side, and various garments and accoutrements spilled over every available area.

"It is not always this much of a shambles. Only my sewing things had been moved here from the small room downstairs."

Annabel's tone was defensive, and an unlooked-for resentment made him speak curtly. "What you mean is that you displaced it to accommodate me."

"Well, yes, but it is no great matter."

"You need not bend over backwards to be amiable, Annabel." This was beyond what he could endure. Let them be done with it! "Open the box."

She did so. There were but two coins remaining. Hal was about to drop the handful of money inside when the box itself caught his attention. It was green in colour, with a pattern of flowers painted on the sides. He reached out and took it from her, half-closing the lid to look at the top.

His breath caught. Just as he had suspected! He had given her this upon the occasion of their betrothal. He'd purchased it to house his real gift—a string of pearls. The box had been lined with rose silk.

He remembered this just as he looked up and caught Annabel's eye. Her lips were trembling, and there was a light in the green gaze that had the most disturbing effect upon his pulses. Her tone was hushed.

"The lining became worn, so I removed it. I sold the pearls to buy Rebecca's cradle, and other things she needed."

But she had kept the box! A faint stirring of hope stilled his senses. She had not forgotten what there had been between them. It had become overlaid with bitterness, but she had not forgotten.

"Hold it open."

He dropped the coins inside. Annabel took the bills, folded them and placed them carefully inside, but she removed several coins and stashed them under her pillow.

"I like to keep a little by in case Janet should need money urgently."

He watched her replace the box in her hiding-place, and a slight warmth grew in his breast at the thought that she did not try to conceal it from him.

Hal turned and left the room, waiting for her at the top of the stairs. He let her precede him down.

Annabel turned to him as he reached the bottom. "Why have you hired the Empty House? Oh, I know what you told Mr Maperton, but you will not fob me off with that tale."

A faint smile crossed Hal's lips, and he moved towards the front door. "It was only half the story, I grant you. Do you care to go over and look at the place?"

"Why, Hal?" she persisted. "Why have you taken it?"

"Whether I go or stay, Annabel, you shall not remain in this hole. I am determined on that at least. But since I am forced to believe that you had rather remain in Steep Ride than go elsewhere with me, it behoves me at least to place you in more worthy accommodation. The Empty House is close enough to what you know, and may certainly afford you greater comfort—given that its faults are corrected."

Annabel followed him out of the cottage, her heart sinking with a dreadful realisation. She did not wish to live in the Empty House! What she wanted more than anything in the world was to leave Steep Ride—with Hal.

Chapter Seven

Hal had been gone two weeks. Restless, Annabel prowled the bare rooms of the Empty House, feeling all the force of its living up to its name.

Unable to settle, nor to concentrate her mind on any of the tasks that awaited her attention, she had opted to go to her proposed new dwelling to decide how best its chambers might be apportioned. She had offered to take Becky, but her daughter, whose attachment to Kitty was total, had revolted upon hearing that the kitten might not accompany them. So Annabel had gone alone.

The house was cold, despite the heat of the day, and she shivered a little in the thin white muslin. Its echoing chambers had the effect of making Annabel feel forlorn. It was a good deal bigger than End Cottage, with three more rooms, each of them larger than Annabel's family room at home. But the walls were peeling, the ceilings cracked, and all the woodwork looked dull. Hal had suspected wood-beetles.

"But that may be remedied," he had said, running a hand down the banister. "What may be found to be more unmanageable is if the wet has got into the rafters."

The inspection undertaken by his batman, however, had been halted. Two days after the visit of Mr Maperton, Hal had announced at dinner that he was going away.

Shock had sent a flurry of dismay through Annabel's pulses, and she had dropped her fork.

"Going away! When?"

"Tomorrow morning."

She had stared at him, a riot of hideous confusion in her mind and heart. She had been too unforgiving! She had driven him off with her temper and the ill-considered bitterness of her remarks. He could not endure it, no matter how he cared for Rebecca. She had known he did not care for her! She had wished him otherwise so many times. But faced with the prospect of his leaving, she was distraught. Barely could she command her voice to utter the thoughts crowding to be said.

"I suppose I cannot blame you. I had not thought it would come to this."

Hal had frowned a moment. "What are you talking about?" Then his brow had cleared. "Devil take it, do you think I mean to desert you?"

She had drummed her fingers on the table. "But you said you are leaving."

He had reached out and stilled her restless hand with his own. "If you were not so quick to take me up, I would have gone on to say that I will be back in a week."

Annabel had eyed him, unable to prevent a churning fear that he was lying. Hal had evidently seen it, for he had removed his hand and sat back, his brow lowering.

"You don't believe me."

She had looked quickly away, ashamed to confess it. "Time will prove me wrong, I hope, if that is so."

"*If* it is so!" He had leaned his elbows on the table, loosely clasping his hands together. "I wish you might find it in you to trust me. After all that has been said between us, do you truly think I would leave for good without discussing the matter with you? I should have thought my feelings had been known to you by now."

Which, Annabel reflected, had been precisely

the difficulty. She did not know his feelings. At least, she knew them in regard to Rebecca. As to herself, she was convinced that his first impression of her had stuck. He had said now and then that she had not changed as much as he had thought at the outset. But he had never said that there remained a vestige in him of the love he had once felt.

Hal had gone on to state only that he had business to attend to. He said nothing of its nature.

"But you may depend upon it that I will be back."

Yet the week's end had come and gone, and brought no Hal. Annabel's spirits, which had plummeted immediately upon his departure, had sunk lower still. She had run the gamut of reaction, from cursing him for a liar and a cheat to trying to persuade herself that she was glad.

The only diversion that had temporarily offered had been the arrival of Athene Filmer and her betrothed. With them had come—entirely unexpectedly and generally incognito—the Duke of Inglesham. At first Annabel had known nothing of his arrival, for though Athene came to visit and Annabel was among those privileged to meet Nicholas Cameron, no word had been spoken of the gentleman who had accompanied them.

But a flustered Charlotte had escaped to Annabel's cottage, there to pour out to her most trusted friend both the gentleman's identity and a history that came as no surprise.

"I must speak of it to *someone* or I shall burst. You of all people will not judge me, I know, dear Annabel." Her gentle features had grown pink. "Inglesham is Athene's father!"

A flurry of tears had accompanied this confession, and Annabel had thrown aside her own concerns to offer comfort—which was, she had soon discovered, unnecessary.

It appeared that the Duke, a widower, had not only been instrumental in bringing the young couple together, but he was again courting his old love and already talking of marriage.

While Annabel had said all that was proper to the occasion, she could not help indulging in a little envy. Ironic, that she could appease her friend's discomfort so readily, and yet manage so poorly on her own account!

Staring from the front window of the Empty House, across the woodlands through which she could see the chimney of End Cottage, she was forced to realise at last that the forlornness that had attacked her in this place had its origin in Hal's continued absence. Fiercely, she lashed herself aloud.

"Fool! Will you confess that you are missing him? Will you pretend that his presence is necessary to your comfort, when you have managed these three years without him?"

Had it been only her bitterness against him that had sustained her? Without it, was she disarmed against the resurgence of the feelings that had driven her into the mad passion that was the origin of her troubles?

No, for she did not love him! The feelings she cherished now had nothing to do with that violent pull of attraction she had felt as a girl of one and twenty. They had fired each other then—in every way. Hal had only to be in the same room with her, and her whole heart and mind had been obsessively attuned to his. And he had felt it as strongly as she. Or so she had believed then.

But now—! Here her thoughts suffered a check. She leaned her forehead against the windowpane, as if in its cool glass she might solace the desperate need that opened an aching void inside her. And now? God, but she did want him!

She recalled the kiss he had given her in the heat of battle. At the time it had registered only as a periphery, but in the far reaches of her mind had sparked the memory, driving down into her loins. She had known him once, and despite every valid reason to crush it out of existence, the knowledge was still with her. And it made her yearn.

Jerking abruptly from the window, she pushed herself into motion, walking swiftly away to the front door and letting herself out of the house. She must not think of these things! If he had gone for ever, she would regret such thoughts a thousand times. She would be better employed in rehearsing a reason for his departure that would convince her acquaintance more strongly than the one she had already used.

Forced to account for Hal's absence to too many questioners, she had outworn his own excuse. He had business in another part of the country. What should she say, if he never returned? That she was again a widow? He had said it in jest, but she would use it if he betrayed her now!

She was already inclined to skip the service at Abbot Giles tomorrow, for fear that people might eye her askance if she again appeared without her bogus husband.

As it was, her ingenuity was called upon sooner than she thought for. Approaching the cottage from the back way that led to the Empty House, Annabel espied a female form in a familiar-looking figured gown. It must be Jane's Saturday off! In her pre-occupation, she had forgotten.

The schoolmistress waved, and came towards her. "I was coming to look for you, for Janet said you were up at the other house. Are you going to move in there?"

As she explained the proposition, Annabel led her back to the cottage. Janet was requested to prepare lemonade, and the two ladies went into the garden where Rebecca immediately showed off her kitten. Miss Emerson, who had seen it that first day, exclaimed upon its growth and bestowed suitable praise upon Kitty's beauty.

"Well, Rebecca is evidently happy," commented Jane Emerson, throwing herself down upon the grass, heedless of the possibility of stains upon her cotton gown.

Annabel was aware of question in her friend's gaze as she followed suit, and made a business of arranging her muslin petticoats in order to avoid Jane's glance. In vain.

"I wish I might say the same of you, Annabel."

"I don't know what you mean."

"Then why are you fidgeting?" Jane let out her merry laughter. "You forget my calling, Annabel. I am adept at reading people."

Annabel drew a breath. "Well, and what are you reading?"

Jane smiled. "Captain Lett is not yet returned, I take it. Oh, you need not conceal your chagrin from me, Annabel. Where is the wretch?"

Now was the moment to invent a good excuse. But the temptation to unburden her mind was too strong for Annabel.

"He may be in the Antipodes, for all I know!"

Jane burst out laughing. "Oh, dear. I had a notion all was not as it should be between you."

"No, and I dare say you are not the only person," said Annabel tartly. "And if it is as I suspect, and he does not mean to return, I don't know what I am to tell people."

"Fiddle! Why should he not return? I take it you have quarrelled, but—"

"Incessantly! Oh, it is too bad, Jane. You do not know the whole, and I cannot tell you, but believe me, I am almost at the point of wishing that he had not come back."

Jane's laughter was quenched, and she laid a hand on Annabel's arm. "You do not mean that, I am persuaded. You are missing him, are you not?"

"Like the devil!" uttered Annabel on a sudden burst of sobs.

The weakness passed swiftly, sped on its way

by the hideous realisation that it was true. Besides, the sound had attracted the attention of Rebecca, and Annabel was obliged to allay her alarm by pretending that she had merely had a coughing fit.

"Mama is all right, darling. Go and play."

Satisfied at length, Becky ran off again to find where Kitty had hidden herself among the banks of shrubs.

Miss Emerson, however, was seriously troubled. "Poor Annabel, it is too bad of your husband to be absent so long. But I dare say he cannot help it. Business so frequently takes a deal longer than one had anticipated."

Annabel sighed. "It is probably foolish of me, but I am having difficulty convincing myself that he will come back."

"Did he say he would?"

"Yes, but—"

"There you are then. This is nothing but an irritation of the nerves, Annabel. Has he taken all his belongings?"

Startled, Annabel looked at her. "I had not thought of that. He took his servant with him, but yes—there are things of his still in the house."

"Then he must mean to return."

It was logical, but the idea, once put into Annabel's head, compelled her to investigate. Jane partook of tea and cakes with them, so that it was three o'clock before Annabel had an opportunity to go into the back room where Hal had been sleeping.

She went in through the parlour door, for since Hal had taken it over, the door through to the kitchen was generally locked from the inside—or so Janet had been heard to say.

As she entered, it was borne in upon her that she had not set foot inside the chamber since Hal arrived. It looked different from how she remembered it. The truckle bed had been set against the far wall, and the table at which she had been used to work was now in the corner opposite. Hal was evidently using it for a desk, for there were piles of correspondence and books laid upon it. The chair was tucked in neatly.

For the rest, there was but a cloak bag, and in the chest which Janet had emptied of her fabrics, Annabel found a collection of Hal's clothing. She was forced to concede that he was unlikely to abandon as many of his belongings as this.

Convinced at last, she immediately began to worry that an accident might have befallen to prevent him from keeping to his time. Only would he not have sent word? By Weem, perhaps, for he could not have need of that ex-batman—whose ser-

vices seemed to encompass groom and valet along
with everything else!—if he was laid by the heels.

Annoyed with herself, Annabel sought for distraction. Crossing to the desk, she picked up the
books and looked at the spines. One was a novel
by Smollett, the other a dissertation on estate management. Annabel flicked idly through the pages,
recalling that Hal had told her he had inherited his
godfather's estate. Was that what was keeping
him? There must have been work to do there, she
supposed. But enough to keep him for two weeks?
August was already fifteen days old!

The books were dropped back on to the table.
Her fingers drummed on its surface, and travelled
along it to the batches of papers. She lifted a doc-
ument, and found beneath it a leather-bound notebook. Catching it up, she discovered it to contain
nothing but accounts.

Disappointed, Annabel went to return it to the
pile, and paused. Her eye caught upon a package
tied up with cord that had been revealed by the
removal of the notebook. The direction was to
Captain Colton at an army encampment in Spain.
But it was not this fact that had riveted Annabel's
attention. She was staring at the scrawled hand-
writing in which the package had been addressed.
It was a hand she knew as well as she knew her

own. The hand of Benjamin Howes, her own father.

Annabel put out fingers that trembled. Almost without intent, she grasped the package up, lifting it closer, feeling a numbness steal over her.

No, she had not been mistaken. It was Papa's writing!

Suddenly eager, she struggled with the knotted cord. Her fingers had become all thumbs. Frustrated, she dragged the cord off one corner and pulled the package free. In seconds, she had unrolled it, revealing a wad of letters, their seals intact. All were addressed to herself.

Clutching them in one hand, Annabel pulled out the chair without any conscious realisation that she did so, her attention fully on the letters. She sat down and dropped them all but one to the table. Her heart beating like a drum, she broke the seal.

Annabel set down the last of the letters upon the pile she had made to one side. She laid her hand on them, as if by that gesture she might caress the sentiments contained therein. Her heart was too full for her to analyse its contents, and she felt extraordinarily fatigued. It was as though the tempestuous writings, through which she seemed to have lived and died a thousand deaths, had taken her on an exhausting journey through the haunting agony of Hal's despair.

She had no notion of the time, though she supposed it must be late. Her reading had catapulted her through a lengthy year or more, and she felt as if she had lived every day of it in this little time. How closely did his passion mirror hers! From urgent question he had travelled a path of torment and bitterness enough to match her own. And Annabel had wrung her tears again on his behalf.

At the last he had tried, months after receiving back all the rest, to reach her once more. And in that letter he had made the promise which he had now fulfilled.

"Whatever it takes, however long, know this. I shall find you, Annabel, and you shall answer me."

Well, and was he answered now? Between that and his coming, how much time had passed? He had kept his promise, but what of his passion? He had not acted in a fashion indicated by his letters. If his passion was there at all, it had dulled. Or was it merely spent?

Slowly, Annabel began to fold up the letters, handling them with tenderness. She was in the act of wrapping them up again in the paper that had packaged them, when a sixth sense caused her to look up. She froze.

Hal was standing by the half-open door, one hand upon the outside handle. He was still wearing a drab travelling greatcoat, but his hat was in his hand. His gaze was fixed upon the paper under her hand.

Annabel could not speak. Her throat tightened where the blood thrummed, and it was all she could do to contain the impulse to leap up from the chair and back away. Her pulses began to riot and she felt sick.

Hal lifted his gaze from the letters to her face. She had read them, that much was plain. His chest felt hollow. He knew not what to say.

He had driven with a growing eagerness, possessing his soul with as much patience as he could for the inconvenient length of the journey. It had been Annabel's green eyes that beckoned—as they had ever done. The devil, how he had missed her! And much against his will.

But to find her thus engaged—with that in her face which told him she had plainly understood the anguish of his hurt—could not but make him both apprehensive and conscious.

Before he could think how to act, Annabel was rising. In haste, she thrust the half-closed package back to the pile from which she had taken it. He watched her come away from the table, and push back the chair in a manner that clearly signalled her agitation. Then she was confronting him.

"I supposed you had disappeared for good."

Not a word about the letters! He might have known it. Disappointment flicked like a whiplash against his breast. Dully, he answered her.

"I make you my apologies. The business upon which I was obliged to engage occupied more time than I had anticipated."

Annabel could have wept. Had she not known that the expressions of need in those dratted letters had been long ago despatched? She stiffened, taking refuge in pride.

"I dare say I may ask in vain what business it was that kept you so long."

Hal threw his hat on the bed and moved to the desk. With an air of finality, he replaced the notebook over the disturbed letters. He spoke without looking at her.

"It was a family matter."

"Oh, that is most enlightening."

She regretted the caustic note immediately, but it was too late. Hal turned, and his features were grim.

"Nothing has changed, I see. If you really wish to know, I went to my brother Ned. There is work to be done at the estate my godfather left me, and I wished him to act for me and put it in hand. It was therefore incumbent upon me to let him know just what I have found here, and what is likely to happen.''

That the explanation was reasonable, and only what she had expected, did nothing to alleviate Annabel's discomfort. Then his words penetrated, and she leaped in without thought.

''What is likely to happen, Hal? I should be as glad to know that as your brother.''

Hal compressed his lips, with difficulty holding back a retort in kind. As if she was not perfectly aware of the options! He adopted the coolest tone he could.

''I shall refrain from answering that. It would scarce be politic to provoke an argument on my first evening back.''

Annabel walked swiftly to the door. The last thing she wanted was to argue with him. It was only her conviction of his lack of affection for her that drove her to fight. Better to leave him, if she could not control her emotions.

He stopped her as she went through the door. ''Where is Becky? Is she in bed already?''

That Annabel had no notion she felt to be another black mark against her. No doubt Hal thought her the worst of mothers! Then common-sense reasserted itself. Becky could not be in bed, for she would have found her mother to say goodnight. There had never been a single instance when Annabel had not tucked her up.

"Did you not see her on your way in? She is probably helping Janet in the kitchen. Or rather," she amended with an involuntary smile, "she will be helping Kitty to get under Janet's feet."

Hal let out a brief laugh, and felt a slight relaxation of his muscles. He had not realised how stiffly he had been holding himself. Impulsively, he asked the question he might well have asked of Annabel herself.

"Did she miss me?"

Her features tightened. "Why don't you ask her?"

Annabel left him on the words, beset by an unreasoning jealousy. It was plain that he did not care in the least whether *she* had missed him.

The long walk should have refreshed her. She had left Becky at home, for the August heat was unrelenting. The straw hat kept the worst of the sun off Annabel's face, but she felt both hot and sticky with the grime of the roads in her sprigged muslin gown and in her hair. Her sandals, tight from swollen feet, had gathered quantities of dust.

It had been foolish, perhaps, to make the journey to Abbot Giles on foot. Hal had offered to drive her there, but Annabel had refused his aid. She was sorry for it now. It had been one thing walking at nine in the morning, but the chattiness of Miss Lucinda Beattie had kept her past noon. The sun was now high overhead and Annabel felt as if she were wilting.

She had gone to see Miss Beattie only to get out of the house. She had claimed that it had been her custom to visit the gossipy spinster, and that she felt guilty that she had not done so since Hal's arrival. It was a legitimate enough excuse, but she knew it for an excuse.

Not that she needed to get away from Hal, for he spent more time out of the cottage than in it. If he was not fixing something on the exterior of the building, he was away at Abbot Quincey, purchasing supplies or items that he needed for the work he was putting in hand.

Annabel did not think he put much attention on the Empty House, although Weem was now living there. The batman had made enough of a habitable space in one of the upstairs rooms, but he came to End Cottage to take his meals in the kitchen with

Janet. For all Annabel knew, Weem was engaged
in mending and fixing up there just as Hal was
doing at the cottage. What she did know was that
there seemed to be so much work on hand that Hal
never had a moment to discuss anything with her.

If this was to be the pattern of their lives together, then Annabel wanted no part of it. It was
Friday now, and more than a week had passed
since his return. They had met, if at all, at meals
during that time. Invariably, Hal disappeared with
a candle to his room after dinner, saying he had
accounts to see to or letters to write. Annabel had
found herself torn between distress, rage and a
growing loneliness.

Yet each second of every day, despite the lack
of communication between them, Annabel was
acutely aware of his presence. She *felt* him, even
when he was not immediately visible. She could
not settle to her work without feeling herself tense
up in anticipation of his sudden entrance where she
was. And whenever he did appear, she clammed
up for fear of betraying the effect of his coming
upon her unruly pulse.

The situation had become intolerable. Hence her
visit today to Miss Beattie. But the plan had mis-
fired. All that Luncinda Beattie wanted to talk
about was the restoration of her husband. If she

commented once upon his handsome looks and dashing moustache, she must have done so fifty times! Annabel could willingly have strangled her.

But now the way seemed tortuous, for all the straightness of the road. She was thirsty, and the sound of oncoming horses and a vehicle made her curse. More dust to be endured!

But when the carriage came into sight, she was surprised to see that it slowed. In a moment, it had drawn abreast, and Annabel recognised the driver.

"What in the world are you doing here, Weem?"

"The guv'nor says as how it's too hot for walking. He sent me to get you, missus."

Annabel's gratitude, as she climbed into the phaeton, was tempered by the realisation that Hal had not come himself. Which only demonstrated how little he cared to be with her. There was clearly too much closeness for his taste in the intimacy of a carriage.

Weem drove on to a suitable turning place, and it was not long before they had turned off the road, and were bowling past Aggie Binns's little cottage with the familiar whites hung out to dry, and on to the track that led past the green.

Annabel thanked her rescuer, and went inside to remove her hat. Her hair was damp with sweat, and a wash in the basin did little to improve the stickiness that clung.

There was nothing for it. She would have to make use of the bathtub. She sighed, for the paraphernalia involved in taking a bath was excessive in this confined space. Janet would need warning, too, for the great tin jugs must be filled with water and set upon the stove for several hours.

She went downstairs in search of her maid, and discovered her directing operations in the kitchen. Young Nat, an insouciant lad of some sixteen years, with a cheery way about him, was hefting a quantity of pots and pans from about the stove and laying them on the big kitchen table. Annabel glanced around at the disarrangement.

"What's to do?"

Janet paused. "The Captain plans to check this stove, for he thinks he can stop the smoking and make it burn stronger."

Annabel blinked. So much for her bath. But something was missing here. "Where is Becky?"

It was Young Nat who answered. "You don't want to worry about the nipper, mum. She's out wi' the master, watching him chop the wood."

Drawn like a magnet, Annabel went out through the back door, and followed into the vegetable garden the regular clunk identifiable as an axe taken to wood. She stood transfixed, prey to a burning sensation that made her mouth dry and her limbs weak.

Before the wood pile—until this moment Young Nat's sole domain—was Hal. He was stripped to the waist, and a ripple of muscle accompanied each lift and swing of the axe. His bronzed torso gleamed sweat, and the red of his hair flamed in the sunlight. Annabel drank in the sight, and the pulsing in her veins was accompanied by a physical ache in that secret place, store of her most guilty dreams.

She did not even see Rebecca, was not aware of her until the child called out to her.

"Mama!"

Hal halted in mid-swing, and stood poised, his eyes seeking for Annabel. He found her, took in her condition in a single glance, and was swept with a coursing fire that leaped down his body and erupted into life.

For what felt an age, his eyes locked with the vibrant green gaze, and every question he had ever asked was answered.

With care, he brought down the axe, jutting it into a log so that it stayed erect. Had instinct had its way, he would have seized her there and then, driving her down and taking her in the swell of heat and sweat.

But Becky was running to meet her, grasping her around the knees. And then Annabel had picked her up, and the moment had passed. Sanity returned, and Hal, his mouth dry, turned aside to pick up his shirt and slide it over his head.

Annabel was coming towards him, Becky in her arms. The light had dimmed a trifle in her eyes, but it was still there. Then she was before him, and the air between them felt charged. She was hatless, without a cap, the dark hair untidy and straggly from the heat. With difficulty, Hal fought down the rise of desire. When she spoke, her voice held a note of hoarse expectancy, like a violin string waiting to be plucked.

"I was going to ask Janet to prepare water for a bath. Only I gather you are to fix the stove."

The meaning of what she said was clear to him, but the tone of her voice permeated his brain, wreathing his senses. He answered, but he felt divorced from what he said.

"If I can find the fault, you may easily take a bath later."

"Oh, no. The water takes hours to heat."

"Not if I can get the wood to burn stronger. It should become a very furnace."

The word struck Annabel with the force of a firecracker. The furnace was already alight. She felt it, and she knew that Hal did also. If only she had the courage to invite him! Only how could she do so? In the middle of the day, and with his plans already laid. She would make herself a wanton.

There was nothing for it but retreat.

"I had better let you get on with your work."

He caught at her arm as she turned to go. "Wait!"

She looked at him in mute question. Hal's gaze dropped to her lips. They were slightly parted, and the invitation was implicit as the tip of her tongue just moistened them. He wondered how he could ever have thought her sensuality to have dissipated. She was everything she had ever been—and more. His finger came up and gently caressed her lower lip.

"*Later.*"

The implication sent colour flying into her cheeks. All too aware of Becky on her hip, Annabel dragged her gaze from his, and turned away towards the house.

True to Hal's words, the stove blazed so that drops from the huge jugs of water sizzled where they fell. Working with Young Nat, who acted as his assistant, handing tools and aiding in the process of dismantling, Hal had readily found the fault. Becky had been fascinated, and Janet had stood by, offering by turns advice and pessimistic warnings of failure.

Annabel had never been so restless. She had wandered in and out, unable to see anything with any clarity except Hal. Hal's limbs; Hal's broad back; Hal's brawny arms. His vibrant hair, and the fluidity of his movements. The very timbre of his voice hummed in her senses.

But as time passed, and Hal's attention remained fixed upon his work, the power of her sensual energies began to dissipate. By the point of completion, when Hal relit the fire and it was seen to roar cleanly into the chimney, giving forth a heat unparalleled since she had first come to the cottage, Annabel had all but abandoned hope of fulfilment of the promise contained in Hal's one word.

It was too late, she told herself. The moment could not be seized, and there was an end. When Hal himself set the big jugs on to boil for her bath, she was conscious only of his attention to the matter at hand. He did not look at her with that same thirsting need!

Nevertheless, the bath—of which she partook in the kitchen in the late afternoon with Janet in attendance—was welcome. She felt refreshed, and almost able to forget what had earlier occurred. Until she heard Hal request Janet to leave the tin bath in the kitchen, so that he might take a bath himself once everyone was in bed.

He had washed outside a little before they dined, but Annabel could not but wonder if he chose to cleanse himself more thoroughly in anticipation of that which she was forcing herself to forget.

At dinner, which they ate earlier than usual, Becky was allowed to stay up. Which gave Annabel an opportunity to keep her attention on the child. She felt foolishly conscious, apprehensive that Hal would pursue it. More apprehensive that he would not. Nothing was said, nothing hinted at. And with the meal over, she dared not glance at him.

"I will take Becky to bed."

"Yes, and I must see whether Janet has got the water on for me," he responded, rising from his chair.

Annabel hid in her chamber, once she had tucked Rebecca in. What was she to do? Was it over? Should she go to her bed and sleep? Sleep! How would she sleep, with the churning question raging in her loins?

She heard at length Janet coming up the stairs, and slipped out of her chamber.

"Is the master having a bath?"

Janet nodded. "I gave him an extra saucepan of water or two. After what he did, I told him he can have all the baths he wants."

Annabel retired to her room again, pacing along the side of the bed and back again. What should she do? With an air of determination, she undressed herself and put on her nightgown. But she did not get into bed. Instead she sat on its edge, her mind raging with images. And all the while there was Hal downstairs—naked in the bath. She found that she was shivering, though the night was warm.

At length, she could no longer bear it. Slipping out of her chamber, she crept down the stairs. Sounds from the kitchen indicated that Hal was still bathing. Stealthily, Annabel moved to the kitchen door and quietly turned the handle. It did not squeak as she half expected. The thought wafted vaguely through her mind that none of the doors squeaked any longer.

But as she pushed it open, her mind blanked of all thought. Hal was standing on a mat next to the bathtub, having evidently just climbed out. He had a towel across his back, which he was rubbing vigorously. But from Annabel's perspective, every aspect of his manly body was open to her view.

Her mouth dried. Then the towel stilled as he saw her. He made no attempt to cover himself as their eyes met.

Annabel could not move. Slowly, Hal began to use the towel again, absently, as if he had no attention on what he was doing. The strong, muscled lines of his body shifted in ripples which drew Annabel's gaze. And the rise of his need sent a pulsing energy dancing down her loins.

She closed the door, leaning against it. She did not know how she remained upon her feet, for her limbs felt as if they were jellied.

Then Hal spoke, his voice guttural with anticipation. "Are you sure you want this, Annabel?"

From somewhere she found strength to utter. "If I did not, I would not have come to you."

For a moment longer, he did not move. Then he suddenly threw the towel aside. Annabel started forward even as he took the first couple of steps. The next instant, she was crushed against the bare length of him, and his mouth closed over hers.

Chapter Eight

The kiss was explosive. Heat radiated from his flesh, consuming her thoughts in a simmering ferment of fever. Her mouth moved under his, and the taut lines of his back rubbed fire into her questing hands.

His mouth left hers, and she arched her neck to receive the blazing trail of his lips within the hollows there. She felt his fingers driving over the thin fabric of her nightgown, burning her through its folds. He grasped her buttocks in both hands and thrust her pelvis hard against his own.

A hoarse rasp of passion left her throat as she felt him, hard and ready, the master of her nightmare need. Once had she known him, and the memory had lingered in her dreams. So close now, so real again.

She murmured his name, and felt him tugging at the intervening cloth that held him from his purpose. His lips engaged her own again, and Annabel's loins screamed for mercy. Her breath was thick, her brain wreathed in a febrile tempest that made her cling and press—nay, demand!—that thorny passage to the chasm of her need.

And every motion, every ardent call was answered, doubly fierce and fervent—with his limbs, with his fingers, with the whole hard muscled maleness that was Hal.

Annabel felt the door against her back, his hands below her thighs. His fingers trespassed, and she gasped as the heat redoubled there. Hal seized her mouth again, while his hand took guidance of the weapon into that niche he had long ago claimed his own. He stabbed, and cried out even as her moan of anguish breathed fire into his neck.

Again he pierced, driving the shaft into the pit, and the flame and throb of his senses was echoed in the plaintive sounds she made. He whispered her name, and her mouth snaked up to find his lips, devouring deeply of the velvet storm. The tang and savour of him drowned her, and the hard feel of him within caused a swelling agony that made her writhe and tremble with arousal.

Hal shuddered into her, lifting her at the thighs

that he might quicken to her need, as ardent as his own. Wild and fierce his thrusts, making of her well a very furnace.

Annabel was helpless, abandoned to his motion. Her hands gripped his arms where the rock-hard muscles stood out, and her teeth bit into his shoulder. But there was no quarter, no mercy, as the dizzying shudders drove the blood up, up into her head. Nothing was real, nothing mattered save the pounding palpitations and her breathless, heaving answer.

Abandonment was all there was. And then an eruption so intense that all thought vanished utterly.

At length she came aware, and the sound of Hal's ragged breath was in her ears. She was hard against the door, and sagging in his slackened grip. She felt her legs released and her feet once more touched the cold stone flags of the kitchen floor. But his arms supported her still, though his head drooped against her own.

Her eyes opened and met the blue-grey gaze, cloudy now. He kissed her lips—a light caress—and shifted back. A laugh panted out of him.

"That has been a long, long time overdue."

Annabel had not breath to respond. Her hands lingered on his chest, and her fingers came in contact with the fine adorning curls, redder than his own hair. She smoothed them absently, and reached up a stealthy hand to run a finger over his lips with delicate touch, feeling the coarser line of his moustache.

She became aware of his gaze upon her. Meeting his eyes again, she found them questioning. Her lips curved in a smile.

"It is like a dream."

Hal nodded. "One that has haunted me these three years."

She made no answer, and his fingers curled into one of her loose black tresses. Now, in the aftermath of their frantic coupling, she seemed not to have changed at all. Perhaps it was the hair, loose about her shoulders.

In the old days when first they courted, the dark future unheeded or unknown, they had escaped once to the country—an illicit day, unchaperoned. He smelled again the odour of fresh cut hay that had been in the air, mingling with the remembered scent of Annabel herself as he had held her close. He might have taken her then, but her innocence and trust had held him back, more perhaps than his gentlemanly instincts. She had loosened her hair and let it fly free.

It was a picture he had carried with him. The

green eyes glinting at him in the features that ever mirrored her sharp intelligence; the straight dark locks blowing in the wind, and the muslins that clung about her slim form.

His heart swelled. Without warning, he slid his arms under her and picked her up bodily from the floor.

"What are you about?" uttered Annabel, between surprise and alarm.

"I am taking you to my bed. This time, I want more of you than one stolen fumble in the dark."

Annabel slid her arm about his neck and sank into his chest as he began to walk with her towards the door that led from the kitchen into his downstairs room.

"If that is your name for it, sir, I can only wonder at what awaits me now!"

For answer, Hal dipped his head to kiss her lightly, and it was with pleasurable anticipation that Annabel presently settled beside him. Not in the confined space of the truckle bed, but upon the floor where Hal dragged the mattress. Her limbs entwined with his, and she gave up her mouth, long thirsty, to this nectar drink.

Annabel woke in the early hours of Saturday morning, and found Hal sleeping heavily at her side. The night's doings were recalled to her mind. In the stark cold of the approaching morn, her passion dulled with satiation, she roved the memory for words that should have been uttered. They were not there to be found.

He had not said it! In all the fervid writhings of the night, there had been no mention of love. He had taken her again, gentling her this time, lingering over the act as though he must imprint each instant in his mind. His every motion had been redolent of affection, but he had said naught.

To what then had she given herself? The coupling had, she knew, been the culmination of a build-up over these several days. She had not known it, but it was evident that Hal had been as aware of her as she of him. Was it then only the proximity of his maleness that had permeated her with that tinder to flare into a raging fire? Had he been moved to it by the intensity of their quarrels?

His experience, his knowledge, was there in each fondling instant, every deep caress. Were there beauties then in Spain for his delight? Had he pleasured them with as much dedication as he had shown to Annabel herself? How was she to know?

Had he spoken one word, had he but uttered one endearment—she would have taken it for her own.

And if there was no affection, then Hal had used her, as he would use a whore.

Her mind froze on that thought. They were yet unmarried. God, but she had forgotten! In the wash of her desire, there had been no hint of recollection of the falsity of her state. Almost she had come to believe in Captain Lett! But Hal was not Captain Lett. He was Captain Colton, and though the father of her child, he was not her husband.

And Annabel had given herself to him—without one word said of love.

Desolation filled her breast, and she slipped quietly out from under the covers. In the grey gloom that crept in from behind the curtain, she sought for her nightgown. Clutching it to her, she made stealthily for the door to the kitchen, and padded softly back to her own bed, there to lie wakeful and lonely, a prey to remorse.

He could not believe it. How could she be so withdrawn from him? After what they had shared, Hal had imagined all would now be well again. A foolish supposition, as it now appeared.

Annabel had greeted him with reserve at breakfast, unable to meet his eyes. For a moment or two he had taken it for shyness. But that was not like Annabel. Certainly not the Annabel of last night, who had matched him with fervid heat, tangling with him in as loose an ecstasy as his own.

She concentrated her attention on her daughter, and spoke to him only at need. What ailed her? It had been bad enough that she was gone from his bed when he awoke. He would have reached for her and taken her again. Deprived, he had sighed his frustration, supposing only that her maternal cares had intervened. It had not crossed his mind that she had left him for reasons of her own— unfathomable.

No, it was not shyness that caused her to break away when he would have touched her with that caress of ownership to which last night had made him heir. Hurt and bewildered, Hal sought for a moment when he might question her in privacy.

But Annabel was determined to avoid his catching her alone, it seemed. It was not until near noon that he found a break between chores and discovered her at work in the vegetable garden. She was digging with concentrated attention, and the sight of her in that dreadful faded gown, attacking a task that she no longer needed to perform, set the seal on his resentment.

Annabel found herself rudely seized, and dragged up from where she had been kneeling. She gasped with shock, and tried to pull away from Hal's strong grip upon her arm.

"No, you don't!"

"Release me at once! How dare you attack me in this way?"

"How dare you treat me to this coldness?" he returned angrily.

Her cheeks flew colour, and she dropped her gaze from his. "I don't know what you mean."

He released her, putting her roughly from him. "Don't dissemble! Of all things, I have not deserved that of you."

Annabel bit her lip, her eyes seeking this way and that for a way of escape. She could not answer him. How was she to speak the doubts in her mind? How ask him for an avowal of affection which he did not feel? She muttered the only thing she could think of.

"We made a mistake."

"A mistake! The devil fly away with you, Annabel! This goes beyond what I may tolerate."

His tone jerked her into resentment. Her eyes came up to his, sparkling with wrath. "Are you now the arbiter of what I say and do in my own house?"

Hal seized her shoulders and shook her, too angry for circumspection. "You came to me,

Annabel! You let down the barriers. You invited me to partake of your lust!''

It had needed only that. Annabel wrenched herself free. Her voice was shaking. ''Oh, that is your word? I knew it. You made me wanton once, and that is all I am to you.''

''Is that what this attitude denotes?'' He could not believe his ears. ''By God, Annabel, you have accused me once too often! Believe what you will of me, for I care not.''

He turned to walk away from her, his shoulders stiffly erect within the concealing folds of his shirt, for he had been working in shirtsleeves and buckskins. Annabel felt a wrenching at her heart. Without thought, she darted after him.

''Hal!''

He was too upset to listen, and he did not check. Annabel grasped his arm, dragging at it to halt him. He stopped, but he brushed her off, such a blaze of fury in his eyes that she wanted to cry out against it.

''Hal, wait! I didn't mean it.''

His chest was heaving with the rapid cut and thrust of his breath in his throat. He wafted a hand, as if to silence her. He shook his head, his voice harsh.

''It is of no use. I have been a fool. I thought I

could make it work again. But this is beyond what I can endure.''

Despair swept through Annabel. ''Pray, Hal—''

He threw up a hand. ''Don't say any more! You read the letters, Annabel, yet you have been blind to my hurts. Well, I am unable any longer to put your hurts ahead of mine, and that is all. It is over.'' He drew a painful breath. ''You need not fear. I will ensure that all is secure here before I go. But there can be nothing more between us.''

She watched him walk away from her, numb with disbelief. It could not be happening. Had she driven him away at last? From somewhere deep inside, the knowledge came that this was what she had been doing from the first. But it was not the result she had wanted. With a sense of shock, she recognised that all her actions had been taken with but one intent. To test his loyalty. To try his love.

With a corroding sense of failure, Annabel saw that she had lost. The wound was too deep to be felt. It crouched, shadowing her mind. But the love she had deemed dead was found to be encysted in a corner of her heart. Had been so. For it had broken loose again—too late.

Aggie Binns was the last person Annabel wished to see on this appalling day. Her mind was dull with weight of woe, and it was as much as she could do to take in anything ordinary of what was said to her, let alone follow the gossipy mouthings of this wizened little creature who sat in her kitchen, partaking of a glass of ale.

"'Tis a tale o' murder fit to clip the one we knows of, mistress," said she, sharp black eyes snapping. She thrust her face up at Weem, who was seated to one side of her. "And ye can tell her as 'twas ye as brought me here to tell it straight."

Weem grinned. "That's because I've a mind to hear your version, to see if it marches with mine."

Aggie cackled, glancing about at the audience gathered in the kitchen to hear her. Only Janet, who had taken Becky out for a walk immediately upon spying Aggie approaching, was absent.

"I'll not have her scaring the child to death, like she does the rest. A regular witch she is, brandishing that wooden laundry spoon of hers, and shrieking at the village children fit to frighten them into next week!"

Annabel had been relieved. She only wished she might herself have run away. She moved to the table, avoiding contact with Hal, who was standing near the dining-room door—which Annabel was unable to look at without recalling last night's frantic coupling and its hideous sequel this morning.

She sat down opposite Aggie. "Well? And why do you come to me?"

"T'ain't ye, mistress," scorned Aggie. "'Tis the master. Leastways, 'tis his man here which is poking his nose into things as don't be his to know of."

"You cut line, old witch, or I'll hold yer head under yer own pump!" promised Weem. He looked at Annabel. "I'd a notion you'd want to know, missus, seeing as how you've bin here all along."

"Well?" Annabel repeated, too dead inside to be able to summon up any real show of interest. She was aware of Hal behind her. They had met at luncheon perforce, although Janet had told her that he had been out ever since that hateful parting. Annabel had stolen a glance at his face, and found it impassive. He had behaved as normal, but for a stiffness of manner and a hard look in his eye. He had replaced his green frock-coat, a formality which made him more unapproachable.

Annabel had felt crushed, and it had been all she could do to address herself even to Rebecca in her habitual tone.

Aggie had begun her tale, and she forced herself to listen. It appeared that Solomon Burneck had fulfilled his promise to tell all he knew.

"Tale go back nigh twenty year. "Twere eighteen-ninety-three when it happen. "Twere how yon Abbey were won by the markiss from that other Earl o' Yardley, him as killed hisself that same night."

Hal stepped up to the table, keeping his distance from where Annabel sat. He still felt deeply wronged, although the violent disturbance of his mind had settled. He had fled to the Empty House, where the absence of Weem had enabled him to pace and pace, bursting with the sheer anguish of it all.

Afterwards, he wished he had not left Annabel in so precipitate a fashion. He knew he must have hurt her, but his own need had been paramount just at that moment. But he was determined not to re-open the discussion. Her conduct had convinced him that nothing could eradicate the bitterness those three years had wrought. Had it been possible, he would have left the place at once, for to be in her company now was a species of torture. Especially after last night, the memory of which charged him even now with renewed desire, the worse for knowing it could never more be quenched.

He cared little for whatever it was the laundry-woman had to tell, but he could see there would be no being rid of her unless she was allowed to speak her piece. But he was beyond understanding what she meant to say. He appealed to his batman.

"What in Hades is the woman talking of, Weem?"

"That part of it ain't nothing new, guv'nor. Seemingly the markiss and the Earl o' Yardley— not this present one, but his cousin—was gambling that night, and the markiss won the Abbey and a deal more besides. The Earl then calls for duelling pistols, and shoots himself in the head. That's how the story goes, guv'nor."

Aggie cackled, setting Annabel's teeth on edge. "But it ain't the truth, master, not by a long chalk."

"According to Solomon Burneck, that is," put in Weem.

"Well, what is the truth?" asked Hal, frowning.

He saw Aggie Binns's black eyes light up. That this sort of gossip was her lifeblood could readily be seen.

"Solomon knows. Solomon seen it all! T'weren't the Earl as shot hisself, no. T'were the markiss as put a pistol to his head."

"*What?*" gasped Annabel, shocked out of her stupor.

"I told ye it were murder, mistress."

"But why? What caused him to do it?"

Aggie launched into her tale with relish. It was difficult to follow the gist of her remarks, but Hal called upon Weem to clarify any points which became too much obscured. But the truth—if it was the truth—was shocking indeed.

Apparently the Marquis of Sywell and the then Earl of Yardley had indeed been playing cards together. But the Marquis had cheated. The Earl accused him, and Sywell hit back with an instant challenge. Both men were drunk—which, Hal reflected cynically, scarce needed to be said!—and decided to settle the matter there and then, instead of waiting for their seconds to arrange it in the time-honoured method of duelling.

This was the point at which the story departed from the norm. Duelling pistols were indeed called for, but the Marquis, instead of fighting in the accepted fashion at a distance of so many yards, had given in to the vicious instinct that had ruled his life. He had, so averred Burneck, overpowered Yardley, put a pistol to his head, and shot him in cold blood.

"But if this is true," uttered Annabel dazedly, "why in the world was it never found out before?"

"Ah, that's where it gets interesting, missus," said Weem, "for it's only this Burneck what

claims to know the truth. He says as how this here
markiss blackmailed him.''

"With what?" asked Hal. "What had he to hold
over him to buy his silence? Was it money?"

Aggie Binns re-entered the lists, sharp eyes
glinting up at him. "'Twere the secret as Solomon
tried to hide, master. Him is son to the markiss,
see. Markiss told him so. Ah, and that he'd a'
telled t'world if'n Solomon told on him.''

"Which would not have suited Burneck," put
in Weem, "because his mother was still alive. He
says he didn't think to speak out after she upped
and died, for he thought as how no one 'ud believe
him. And I should say he's right at that.''

"Only too likely," Hal agreed. "If a word of it
is true, which no one can tell.''

"Ah, put your finger on the nub, guv'nor. It's
Burneck what is under suspicion, and it's Burneck
what come up with this story. I put it to you,
guv'nor. Is Jackson about to believe him? Not for
my money, he ain't.''

Annabel recalled that Jackson was the name of
the Runner who had been sent from Bow Street to
investigate the affair. She remembered Hal saying
that Weem had been taking an interest in it, so she
must suppose he had spoken with the Runner.

"But it's excessively important that they find

out the truth," Hal pointed out, "for if the story is true, then the Abbey rightfully belongs to the present Earl of Yardley."

This point of view turned out to be the major cause of talk among the gentry, as Annabel discovered when Hal drove her to church in Abbot Giles upon the following day.

He had said nothing more than that it behoved them to put in an appearance. Annabel had no desire to show herself abroad, for she was horribly aware of drawn cheeks and shadowed eyes. Whether Hal noticed, she had no means of knowing. She kept her face averted from him whenever she could, fearing that he might comment upon it. One could not weep for the better part of the night without it showing in the morning!

On the other hand, Annabel could think of no legitimate excuse to refuse to go to church. She prepared Rebecca, therefore, and put on her own best gown—the same that she had worn to the fête—and tried not to reflect upon the likelihood that this was probably the last time they would attend Sunday service as a family. More depressing still was the sight of Hal's formal attire, the blue coat enhancing his looks, though the beaver hat concealed his burnished locks.

Annabel had reason to be grateful for Solomon

Burneck's revelations. Thanks to Aggie Binns, the story was all over the district, and nothing else was discussed either before or after the service. The Reverend Mr Hartwell referred to it in his sermon, taking the Bible tale of Cain and Abel as his text. The Earl of Yardley, rather to the disappointment of the congregation, Annabel discovered, was not in church that day.

"If he had been," Jane Emerson whispered, in the general gathering outside after the service, "we could none of us have talked of the affair. What a pity that Mrs Filmer has left the village with her daughter. I am sure she would be so disappointed to miss it all."

Annabel could not subscribe to this view. But then only she knew that Charlotte had been swept off her feet by Athene's father, for the Duke of Inglesham's brief sojourn in the area had been a well-kept secret. Charlotte had reason perhaps to be glad of Solomon's scandalous tidings, for she had evidently escaped the keen eye of Aggie Binns. Annabel was glad that Charlotte at least had been granted her wish to depart from Steep Ride. Would she might do the same!

Not even Jane, far too involved in the news, had eyes for Annabel's wan looks, although she took time to chat a little with Becky, who soon left her to pursue an acquaintance with another small child. But Hal, far less divorced from Annabel's well-being than she imagined, could think of nothing else.

He had not meant to hurt her so badly! If he could only have left at once, he need not endure the sight of her distress. That she was distressed he could not doubt. But he had determined on leaving. If he yearned secretly to abandon his purpose, in the hope that Annabel's affections had reanimated towards him, common-sense told him that he would be living in a fool's paradise. It was better to part, before they hurt each other too much to be able to live together in any semblance of harmony. There had been too much misunderstanding, too much disaster. Such losses could not be made good.

It was with only half an ear that he listened to the speculation that was rife upon this story of Sywell having murdered an earlier Yardley. Some believed, as Weem did, that Solomon Burneck was only compounding his guilt with this trumped-up tale. Others, who cited a string of atrocities to be laid at the door of the Marquis of Sywell, expressed themselves as unsurprised to hear of one more dastardly deed to be set to his account.

Only one thing was plain, as he ventured to

mention—for want of any other safe subject of discussion—when he drove them all home. There would probably never be an answer to the riddle of Sywell's death.

"And the plain truth is," he pursued, "as far as I can make out, that no one in this area wants a solution."

It was not the topic uppermost in Annabel's mind, but she embraced it with relief. At least it offered a chance to converse! Removed from what she truly wanted to talk about it might be, but it was better than nothing.

"What makes you think so?"

"They appear as one to be so grateful to the murderer for ridding the place of its most tiresome encumbrance that they are inclined rather to reward than punish him."

"But the law will prohibit that," Annabel pointed out, straightening Rebecca's bonnet, which had become disarranged by the wind. The little girl was in her element, for she regarded any ride in the phaeton as a high treat.

Hal was in agreement with Annabel. "It is why, I suspect, it is generally agreed that it would be better for the mystery to remain unresolved."

From behind them, Weem interrupted. "Jackson won't stand for it, guv'nor. "Sides, there's the matter o' the ownership o' the Abbey to be set-tled.''

"Yes, indeed," agreed Annabel. "Everyone has been wondering what was to happen to the Abbey."

"If this here story is true," pursued Weem, "then the Earl o' Yardley is going to want to know of it, ain't he?"

"When all is said and done," concluded Hal, "that cannot be gainsaid."

If he had intended to close the subject, he reckoned without Annabel, who forced it to be continued on long beyond natural curiosity could expect, only in order that it might carry them through dinner.

The moment she had said goodnight, and had begun to prepare herself for bed, her mind reverted to the desperate plight in which she found herself. She toyed more than once with the notion of going downstairs again, and seeking Hal out in his little room. But what if he should repulse her? There could be no bearing that! He had made his feelings plain enough, and there was nothing to be done about it.

Yet she continued to churn the matter over in her mind, though she shed no more tears. She felt ill, however, and the suspicion of a headache nagged at her. Her brain ran continually on the horrid question of how long Hal meant to remain. Almost she could wish him gone, so that she need not endure this torture of suspense. Sleep had never been further from her, and she was astonished to wake in the morning and find that she had indeed passed some time in slumber.

Monday brought rain, and the dull skies echoed the desolation that beset Annabel. She was obliged to entertain Rebecca through most of the day, and she told herself she was relieved when Hal went off to the Empty House to see what might instead be achieved there in this impossible weather.

Annabel supposed that he must mean to install her in the new dwelling before he left. Had it not been for the need to maintain an appearance of familial harmony, she dared say he would have moved into the Empty House himself until it was ready for her reception.

She knew not how close to the truth she had come. So hard was it to be in the same house with Annabel that Hal had more than once considered the option of shifting his belongings up the road. But to do so, he must advertise the situation at least to his batman and to Annabel's maid. They might guess at the difficulty, but for him to move altogether must confirm it. He could not subject Annabel to what might readily be taken for an insult.

Yet the situation was highly detrimental to his peace of mind. He must lie below stairs, picturing Annabel in her nightgown sleeping above, remembering in vivid detail the contours and outline of her flesh under his hand. It was worse, having known her again, than it had been before. Bad enough then, when his unruly loins had tugged at him, setting him afire at the motions of her body as she moved about the house.

He had all but forgotten—forced himself to forget!—how sensual were her movements. There had been a quality in the set of her head, and the turn of her neck that had empassioned him. But for the eyes, she was no beauty, that he had ever acknowledged. But the sharp attraction of her features could not be denied. The plane of her cheek and the bewitching blackness of her hair had maddened him. And they did so again.

Only in those first few days, before the violence of her passionate anger had erupted to its full extent, had he been deceived into thinking she had changed. Now it was as if the intervening years had never been.

She was the Annabel he had first seen in a

crowded saloon, whose instant impact had never left him. He was as entangled in her allure as he had ever been, and nothing would change it. But he could not live with her bitterness!

There was an edge of tension in the air. Annabel felt it. Instinct—which she was at pains to deny!— told her that Hal felt it too.

It was in the glances he cast at her when he thought she did not see. It was in the tremble of her fingers when she had taken his platter from him at the end of the morning meal. It was in the un- natural heat of the day, a similar heat to that earlier time that had been their undoing.

Two days of rain had given way to a slow build of sunshine. The air had heated overnight, and the early morning mist heralded a day of unparalleled promise so late in the season. For September was almost upon them.

To compensate Rebecca for two days of remain- ing indoors, when even the joys of playing with Kitty had begun to pall, Janet had offered to take her out.

"We'll go to the lake, ma'am. She'll like to pad- dle. That Weem says as he'll come along of us. Not that I want him, but since the Marquis upped and died, you never know who might be lurking in them woods of his.''

The lake was a place of great beauty, formed by the building of a dam in Little Steep, a tributary running from the main River Steep. And a favourite playground of the village children. Partly because it was said to be haunted, and partly for the enjoyment of a bathe in its cool, fresh waters.

Rebecca was ecstatic at the thought of the treat, and Annabel gave permission. It had not occurred to her when she did so that, since Weem was to go too, she and Hal would be left alone in End Cottage. She resolved to keep busy, that she might keep out of his way.

But the rising heat held her attention on his presence. And Hal chose to remain in the house, attending to the casement in the large room, which had long been on his list. Or so he said.

Annabel was engaged with mending linen. She was working at the table, the sewing-box she kept for minor tasks lying open to one side. As she plied her needle, she was all too conscious both of the heat—though she was clad in the lightest of her muslins—and of Hal just outside the casement, in his shirtsleeves to cope with the heat, and busy with a hammer and nails.

The tension grew. Hal cursed himself for his stupidity. Of what had he been thinking? It was near impossible to concentrate his mind. He should have gone elsewhere—the Empty House. Anywhere but here!

Out of the corner of his eye, he saw Annabel slip her needle into the cloth, and stretch. One hand went up to rub at the back of her neck, and she shifted her shoulders, as if in discomfort from the hunched position in which she had been sitting. She was wearing a cap, but several tresses had escaped, lying tantalisingly along the sensual line of her throat. Hal's mouth dried.

He turned his eyes away, but they refused to focus on the work he had in hand. But when he looked again, Annabel had resumed her sewing, her head bent once more over the sheet she was mending. Without will, he stilled, watching the lines of her face, tracing the strength at her brow and the smooth plane of her cheek.

As if she felt his regard, she looked up suddenly. He caught her glance, and could not look away. Devil take it! He should have known this would happen. His loins betrayed him.

Resistless, he left the window, and rounding the house, went in at the back door. Swiftly, he crossed the kitchen, and found Annabel standing, having pushed away from the table, her eyes trained upon the entrance where he stood.

Hal went to her, but he did not touch her. He could see how she trembled, even as he felt the quivering in his own limbs. He muttered the words, hardly aware of speaking.

"You will be my undoing!"

"As you are mine," she answered.

Hal leaned towards her. His fingers came up and touched her cheek, and his lips brushed hers, featherlight.

And then he was kissing her, hungrily, tugging at her mouth. She was in his arms, and he dragged her close against him. But as his lips left hers, her breath caught on a distinct sob. And Annabel was weeping.

His heart melted, and he drew away a little. "Don't! Oh, don't, Annabel!"

"I c-can't h-help it," she uttered chokingly. "You will t-take me, and then you will l-leave me!"

Hal knew not how to answer. His resolve had been crushed, relegated to the back of his mind. But he remembered it now.

His hesitation damned him. Annabel wrenched away from him, and staggered back, half crashing into the table.

"Take care!" he called automatically.

She waved him away as he came forward to assist her. She was fighting with her tears, trying to crush down the thrusting lump that persisted in her throat.

"If you mean to go," she managed to say, "then go! This waiting is killing me!"

It was the first time she had intimated that she minded his going. Hal felt his resolve crumbling, and tried to tighten up against her. But it would not do.

"This is useless, Annabel!"

"I know it," she uttered, and the green eyes turned to him, misery in their depths. "You said so before, and I know I am to blame."

"I didn't mean that," he protested, half wishing he might go to her, but too afraid of letting his emotions get the better of him.

Annabel sank into her vacated chair, dashing with her fingers at the persistent tears, her breath catching as she tried desperately to halt them.

"I d-don't understand you."

With difficulty, Hal held back from her. "I mean that we are both too apt to be passionate. Was it always so? I don't remember any longer."

Annabel shifted her shoulders, too distressed to

catch at his meaning. "What do you want? I don't know what you mean to say to me."

With determination he leaned his hands upon the table. His eyes caught and held hers.

"I mean, Annabel, that we have three years of misunderstanding between us that has driven us apart. And ever since I have come here, neither one of us has tried to talk of it. Or if we have, it has all ended in a quarrel."

Annabel looked at him, and then at the handkerchief he took from his pocket and held out to her. She took it, but she frowned in puzzlement.

"But you are leaving."

A slight smile crossed his lips, and his hand went to finger his moustache. "I am trying to leave."

The tiny leap at her pulse sent Annabel into panic. She must not speak of that faint rise of hope. And she must not weep again! But her unruly breath caught on another sob.

She wanted to sue to him for mercy. She wanted to fall at his feet and beg him to stay. But pride—that fatal Howes pride!—would not permit of a proceeding so prejudicial to her dignity. She veiled her eyes, looking down that he might not see her piteous self-abasement.

Hal saw only her distress, and knew it would be

impossible to leave. There was only one thing for it then. The air must be cleared.

He crossed to the head of the table, and pulled out the chair there. He sat down, and leaning his elbows on the table, folded his hands.

"Come, Annabel. We have both of us a catalogue of complaint and bitterness. Let's have done with it at last. Let us have it out."

Chapter Nine

Annabel crumpled his handkerchief in her hand. Still she did not look at him.

"I am done with quarrelling. I have no heart for it."

A short laugh escaped him. "That I do not believe!" He leaned towards her, as if he would compel her to turn. "I do not wish to quarrel, Annabel. Can we not talk? Must we only curse and revile each other?"

Absently she touched the bulky sheet that she had thrown down in a heap upon the table. Its presence seemed incongruous, and for a moment she could not think why it was there. Then she remembered that she had been plying her needle. She had no idea where it was, for she had not set it neatly in the cloth as she usually did.

Hal leaned across and gave the sheet a shove that sent it flying off the end of the table. Annabel went to catch it, and he seized her hand to stop her.

"Leave it!"

She turned bewildered eyes towards him. "But I was mending—"

"I said, leave it." His grip tightened. "You have no need to mend sheets now. Talk to me, Annabel!"

She winced. "You are hurting me."

His grip slackened, but he did not let go her hand. There was a light in the blue-grey gaze that compelled her attention. But Annabel became lost for an instant in the beloved sight of him. The strongly handsome features, bronzed from the Spanish sun, complemented by the bright red-gold of his curly hair, and the neat moustache that gave him such an air. Like a burnished god! She spoke without thinking.

"I had almost forgotten your incredible looks. Why did you ever choose me?"

"Because of the passion in your green eyes," he answered without hesitation. His gaze roved her features. "Because of what you are, Annabel, and what you do to me."

She stared at him, drinking him in as if she must

look her fill before he vanished away. All her heart
and mind cried out to him, *I don't want you to go*.
But her tongue thickened in her mouth to stop her
saying the words.

His hand about hers made her fingers tingle, and
in her breast there grew an ache that she remembered all too well. The loss of Hal that she had
once endured when she had broken off their betrothal, and which now again threatened her.

And then he released her. She watched him fold
his hands and sink his chin so that the edge of one
thumbnail caressed his moustache. His eyes never
left her face.

"What happened that night, Annabel?"

The transfer of attention was instantaneous. She
was there again in her mind. Huddled in the carriage after she had left him, in mingled shock and
dread at what they had done in a dark summerhouse.

"I told Papa."

Hal's hands dropped to the table. "The devil
you did! He acted swiftly then, for you were not
there when I came in the small hours to hammer
on your door."

Annabel narrowed her gaze, as if her eyes hurt.
"You came to the house?"

He nodded. "I left the party immediately after

you did, and when I got to my lodging I found my orders there. My regiment was leaving for Dover at first light. I don't know what I intended—except to make it right.''

"I wish I had known it! Papa took me home to his estates,'' Annabel explained dully. "We did not even stay to pack, beyond a few necessities. It was given out that I had been taken ill.''

Hal saw the shadows creep into her eyes. So must they have cast a growing pall over her life in the aftermath of that disgraceful act. While he was trying to reach her, with letters that he now knew had never found their destination, Annabel must have been living in a terrible suspense.

"How long was it before you knew—I mean, that we had been unlucky.''

A faint smile wavered on her lips. "Unlucky? Oh, Hal, it was a disastrous turn!''

He grasped her fingers. "I did not intend to belittle its seriousness. But it was an unfortunate chance that you should fall upon the first occasion.''

"So Papa said,'' she agreed. Her gaze met his. "It was not until we knew for certain that he would agree to act.''

Hal frowned, releasing her. "Act in what manner? He made no approach to me, Annabel.''

She shook her head, her fingers beating an irregular tattoo on the polished wood as the new knowledge of her father's perfidy returned to her mind.

"I know that, though he pretended that he had. At first, however, he refused to do so." Her hands came up to slide across her face and down her neck, in a gesture infinitely hopeless. "Even while we waited to know if I was safe—I in a state of growing terror as each day passed and no word came from you—Papa would not send to you. Nor would he permit me to do so."

Hal put a curb upon his tongue, for the urge to attack Benjamin Howes was strong in him. But he wanted neither to alienate Annabel, nor to drive her from this telling. Only now did he realise how long it had needed to be said.

"Did you write to me then?"

Annabel met his gaze. "Not then. I was already distressed that you had not troubled yourself to write. It did not occur to me—it never did, Hal, even afterwards!—to imagine that my own father might withhold your letters from me. Yet now I see that he must have done so from the first."

It was almost impossible for Hal to keep his tongue between his teeth. There was much he might say, but the time was not yet. Instead, he urged her for more details.

"Did your father tell you why he would not take a course that most would take—to call me to account and demand that I take you to wife?"

Annabel sighed deeply. "You know already that Papa was opposed to the match." Painfully, she drew breath, for the truth was as hurtful to her as it must be to Hal. She eyed him. "You will think him mad, I dare say, but Papa declared his determination to endure my disgrace rather than be blackmailed into giving me in matrimony to a man of whom he could not approve."

Hal's lip curled. "It comes as no surprise to me, but let that pass. What did you do?"

She shrugged. "What could I do? It was painful to me to realise that all you had ever said of him was true. That he was ruled by some unreasoning prejudice, and that my happiness was not at the forefront of his mind." Her features became taut. "God knows I have had proof enough of that!"

"It is no satisfaction to me to have been right in this instance. The fact is that I wrote both to you and to him, but the latter letters he must have kept."

"Because you would not otherwise have believed that it was I who had returned them," said

Annabel curtly. "That much I had deduced. I only wish I had realised to the full how malevolent was his determination to keep us apart!"

"Don't blame yourself for that. How should you do so? You cared for him—I dare say you still do."

She shrugged. "I think I both love him and hate him."

As she had felt towards Hal, she might have added. But she held her tongue on the words. That he was encouraging her to talk did not presuppose that he had changed his mind. Though there was so much balm in the disclosure, she realised, that already she was conscious of being freer in her mind.

Hal smoothed his moustache with finger and thumb, a frown gathering on his brow. "It had been my severest concern—that I might have left you with child. When no letter came in answer to mine, I thought it could not have been so. You are not the only one, Annabel, to have supposed it to be impossible that your father could carry his aversion to that extreme."

"Oh, he did not phrase it in a manner that I could understand it to be so!" cried Annabel, a trifle of heat in her voice at last. "No, Hal. He told me instead that as you had not written, it was clear that you cared nothing for your obligations towards me. My pregnancy being confirmed, I was frantic that you should be informed of it. Papa said that I might write to you if I chose, but it was too late to force you to marry me, for he had heard that you had long been abroad with your regiment and…'

Her voice failed with the memory of the deliberate cruelty of her father's words. Hal watched her with pain, and a surer understanding of the reason why he had met with such hostility. His voice was tender.

"What is it, Annabel?"

The green eyes turned upon him, a world of torture in them. "Papa told me of the casualties that were going forward in the Peninsula, and said that it was useless to hope that you would come out unscathed. The likelihood was that you would be killed." She took a steadying breath. "You may imagine how such a supposition struck me."

"In the condition you were in? Yes, by God!"

"It was then I began to write," she told him, breathless now as her tale gathered momentum. "Driven more by the thought of losing you to war—the idea that you might die without knowing…that, I think, was more to me than the predicament in which I found myself."

She felt Hal's hand grasping her own, though she was by now so lost in her memories that she did not look at him.

"I wrote and I wrote. At first I could not believe that you had not replied to me. It did not seem possible that you would desert me, did you once know that I was carrying your child. I believed in you, Hal! I tried to believe, despite that no letters came. I told myself that you had been embattled, in cantonments, unable to send to me. I even began to suppose that you had indeed been slaughtered. I took to searching Papa's news reports for names of casualties. I did not want to believe you could betray me. Little did I know then whose treachery I had to thank!"

As if to underline the start of her doubts, she withdrew her hand from his. "At last I could no longer hold out against Papa's version of events. Repeatedly, he told me that you had never any true intention to marry me, or you would have moved heaven and earth to see me righted in the eyes of the world. He said—a lie, as I now know!—that he had himself written, revealing it as a fault in you that you would not even reply to his personal appeal."

Hal was obliged to clench his fist and teeth to prevent himself from utterance. His fury with

Benjamin Howes knew no bounds. Setting aside what had been done to him, he was appalled at the lengths to which the man would go in his thirst for vengeance. To condemn his own daughter to this life, only to serve his own selfish hatred.

"Besides," pursued Annabel dully, "I was by now more than six months gone, and the resolution of my situation was urgent." She looked at him. "Truth to tell, Hal, I did not care what happened to me then."

"That does not altogether surprise me," he said, rigidly controlled.

"I left the arrangements to Papa. I lived for the last weeks in a remote cottage upon his estates, and Janet only was with me. Other than her, only our doctor knew of my condition. Rebecca was born there, and as soon as I was well, we removed to this place, and I took upon me the name and background that my father had invented."

She fell silent, and Hal said nothing for a moment or two. He was harrowed by her tale, and disgusted by her father's villainy. There was only one thing to be said to Howes's credit, and that was that he had not altogether repudiated his daughter. It was not an unknown course to be taken by fathers whose daughters fell foul of their own passions. That, or force the girl to give up the baby.

But Benjamin Howes had taken a deliberate path, to the detriment of his daughter's honour—and to Hal's own honour too. What it said of Howes's honour was beyond stating. It was time to set the record straight.

"Annabel."

She started, as if she had been deep in thought, her glance flying to his face. "Yes?"

"I can no longer withhold from you what you are entitled to know."

She blinked at him. "What do you mean?"

Hal made a fist and set his elbow on the table, as if by this he might control the churning rage that consumed him.

"I could not tell you before, for I did not wish to add to your store of distress."

Annabel's heart lurched. "You are alarming me dreadfully!"

"I beg your pardon, I do not mean to do so. It concerns your father."

Her eyes dilated. "Is he ill? Is he dead?"

He waved an impatient hand. "Nothing like that. The plain fact of the matter is, Annabel, that there is a reason for your father's prejudice against me. It has to do with my own father, and a long-time enmity between them."

Puzzlement beset Annabel's mind. She was still

immersed in the events she had been relating. "I don't understand you."

"How should you? I did not know it myself until I sold out. My brother Ned told me the story, just as my mother had told it to him when he had discussed with her the break-up of our betrothal."

Annabel waited, a glimmering of understanding in her mind. "Well, and what is the story?"

"It is simple enough, if only the sequel had not been so tragic—for you. Your father once aspired to the hand of my mother. She was Fanny Denton then, and very lovely—as her portraits testify. Both Ned and I inherit our colouring from her. My late father—Ralph Colton, as you know—was a rival suitor. They fought a duel over her."

"And your father won?"

Hal nodded. "Not that it contributed to his winning her. Indeed, Ned says my mother rejected him for having fought at all. But he did win her in the end, for she cared for him. Benjamin Howes, however, could not bring himself to believe that this was so. He tried by every means to endear himself to her, but to no avail. And the plain fact is that your father sanctioned our betrothal because he did not then know who I truly was. It was only when he discovered me to be the son of Fanny Denton—

or rather the son of his old rival Ralph Colton—
that he turned against me.''

Annabel stared at him, stunned by the revelation.
''He must have been bitter indeed!''

''So much so that he did all in his power to pass
that bitterness on to you. Nothing you could have
said or done, Annabel, would have changed him
towards me. As we have seen, he concealed the
fact that I had written, and he suppressed your letters to me.''

''And that is why he had rather have seen me
ruined?''

Hal nodded. ''There is one mitigating circumstance, and one has to give him that. At least he
gave you some form of respectability. Though how
he could condemn you to a life of penury is beyond
my ability to understand!''

But Annabel was curiously comforted. If Papa's
passion for Fanny Denton had been but a tithe of
what she had felt—did feel still!—for Hal, she
could find it in her to pity him. She might not
forgive him, but at least it offered an explanation
for actions which had otherwise no rhyme or reason.

''He must have been mad with jealousy.''

''Mad, yes.''

''If only I had known it!''

Hal grimaced. "Would it have made a difference?"

"To my confusions, perhaps. But I think I would never have guessed that he would go the length of destroying our correspondence in order to keep us apart—not in the extremity that beset me in carrying your child."

His eyes burned. "He destroyed more than our correspondence, Annabel."

She suffered an instant twinge of apprehension. Did he mean to imply that his affection had been equally destroyed? Was she enlightened now, and had found her own love intact—if bruised—while he had grown cold towards her because of it?

"Yes, you suffered too, I know." Her voice trembled. "Your letters..."

"Not that." A waft of his hand waved the letters away. "I should not have left them here for you to find."

"Don't say that! You wanted me to find them. And you were right. It was right that I should learn how deeply you had suffered."

Hal grimaced. "There were times, I don't mind telling you, when I cursed Providence for sparing me in so many bloody engagements. I might have stopped a bullet at any time, and been glad of it!"

She eyed him, a slow thump beginning at her breast. "But not now?"

He met her eyes. "How can you ask me?"

Her lip trembled. "I ask, because I do not know."

Hal stared at her. "Have you run mad? Is it not obvious?"

Obvious! If it were only so. Annabel covered her face with her hands, holding tight against the rising leap of hope.

"Tell me!" he urged tensely.

She dropped her hands to the table, her fingers gripping each other so hard that the knuckles stood out white. How she was to find courage to look at him, she did not know. Closing her eyes, she turned her head towards him, and then opened them again. The frowning demand in his face unleashed her tongue.

"You came here from a sense of duty—of honour! I have abused you, and I have vilified you. But I swear to you, Hal, I did not know why I did so."

"You have told me why this day—it is implicit in what you have said. But that does not explain your meaning!"

"Oh, I can't explain!" she cried despairingly, a little of her fighting spirit creeping back.

"Try!"

He made it a command, and she responded with heat. "If I could, I would, but I cannot find the words!"

"Then search! But do not fob me off with excuses."

She pushed back her chair and rose from the table, agitation overtaking her. How tell him? How *ask* him? Only if she did not find a way, she would lose him! She turned on him to find that he had risen also, moving out into the room as she had done.

"Cut line, Annabel! Will you cease playing games?"

The gruff tone sent her into a frenzy of protest.

"It is not a game! Hal, you came here with I don't know what intent, but when you saw me—" She broke off, whirling away from him to pace between the sofa and the armchair.

"Devil take you!" he swore, closing in on her. "I am of a mind to choke it out of you, if you don't say it!"

Instinct told him she was on the retreat. If he let up now, he would lose her! In a second, he had her by the shoulders. He felt both murderous towards her, and alight with a bounding leap of hope.

God help him, but if this meant what he thought—!

Annabel felt herself wholly in his power. He knew! He knew her mind, and he would force her to say it. The breath shuddered in her throat.

"You thought me changed. You thought me no longer attractive to you. You said it, Hal!"

"You fool, Annabel! Have I not proved to you that it was not so? If I thought it—if you seemed different—it was only your outward appearance. And that is only due to what you have been obliged to make of yourself."

His hands were digging into her shoulders, and she winced. "Hal, you are hurting me!"

His grip did not loosen. "Then stop prevaricating!"

It was too much. She swung into anger, pushing at his chest. "Brute! I wish I had let you go! I had rather endure to live alone, than to live with your pity, and your duty, and your bullying!"

Abruptly, Hal's fingers left her shoulders and caught instead at her face. His lips fiercely seized hers, in a kiss so rough that her brain froze with the shock of it.

He released her mouth, glaring down at her.

"Is this pity?"

She could not answer, for again his mouth

closed with hers, dragging at her lips in a fashion that sent the blood gushing through her veins. She all but swayed as he came away.

"Is this duty? The devil fly away with you for an obstinate fool!"

His hands left her face, and the next instant she was locked in an embrace so tight that she could not breathe. It loosened a little in a moment, and the only thing she was then aware of was the caressing touch of his lips upon her own.

"I am going to take you upstairs to your bed," he murmured in her ear. "And then I'll show you duty!"

Annabel had no breath left either to answer him or to expostulate. But her imagination painted for her the promise in his words, and the warmth flooded through her to the seat of her desire.

But outside the drowning lack of consciousness, an alien sound penetrated, grew stronger, became identifiable. Beyond the confines of the cottage, came the approach of running feet.

An urgency about the noise jutted through her preoccupation with the sensations Hal was arousing. But in a moment, it became clear that he had felt it too.

She was abruptly released, and she opened her eyes to see him moving towards the kitchen.

"What in Hades—?"

A gate slammed out the back, and as Annabel crowded behind Hal's bulk which was blocking the open doorway, she glimpsed Janet flying through the outer door.

"What's to do?" Hal demanded, moving into the room.

Janet was out of breath, and pouring sweat, her neat appearance thoroughly awry, the hat fallen from her head to swing on its ribbon behind.

A sixth sense sent a cold wind of alarm sweeping through Annabel's bosom. "Becky?"

In an instant, she had pushed past Hal and was seizing her maid by her sinewy arms.

"What is it? What has happened?"

"She fell—" gasped Janet, tears starting to her eyes. "Slipped—in the water. Hit her head—or so we think. Weem is carrying her—as fast as his legs can go."

Annabel's heart pumped fleet as the wind, and her head felt woolly. She would have asked the dread question, but that Hal did it for her.

"Is she much hurt?"

"Can't tell, sir," Janet uttered. "She's breathing, but she ain't conscious."

Annabel thought her shock must have shown in her face, for Hal was suddenly beside her, his arm firm in her back, pushing her to a chair. His tone was terse, the soldier in him instantly at work.

"This is no time for fainting. Think, Annabel! Where is the nearest doctor."

Janet answered. "Abbot Giles, sir."

"It's Dr Pettifer," Annabel said, trying to keep her reeling mind intact. "His house is near the Rectory. The Hartwells can tell you."

"Good." Then he was at the door that led to his own room. "I'll take the phaeton and bring him back with me. I must get my coat. Put the child to bed, and keep her warm. If she wakes, give her water—nothing else. Is that understood?"

Annabel rose again and wafted an impatient hand. "Yes, yes. Go!"

He glanced at her, and then at Janet. "Keep your mistress from fearing the worst!" Then he was gone.

Hal paced the length of the table in the large room downstairs. He had come away, for in Annabel's bedchamber upstairs there was not room enough for himself, the doctor and Annabel too.

Becky had been put to bed in the four-poster by the time he returned with Dr Pettifer. The luck had been with him, for the Reverend Mr Hartwell had been at home, and had himself conducted Hal to the house down the road where the doctor happened to have just returned from a visit to a sick patient at a nearby dwelling.

He had not accepted Hal's offer to take him up in the phaeton, preferring to have his groom drive him in his own gig so that he might go elsewhere when he had seen Rebecca. He had listened with grave attention while Hal told him what had occurred, but refrained from giving any opinion.

"Until I have seen the child, sir, I prefer to say nothing. There is no sense in raising spectres where none may exist."

By which cryptic comment he had succeeded in sending Hal ghost-hunting indeed. Until that instant, he had not even considered what might be amiss with his little daughter. He had acted upon the information that she was unconscious after a fall. A condition, in his experience, that called for immediate medical attention.

But as he drove back to Steep Ride, the doctor's gig close on his tail, he found himself imagining every conceivable disaster, and had to exercise the strictest self-control to prevent himself from fearing Rebecca to be already descended into the grave.

The sight of her pale little face lying deathly still on the pillow had sent a shaft of dismay through him as he had ushered the doctor inside the bed-chamber. He had stayed only to hear Pettifer greet Annabel, and begin to allay her alarms.

"Now, Mrs Lett, I am sure you have been worrying yourself into a frenzy. Let me look at the poor little mite, and we shall soon see whether there is any cause for alarm."

Hal had glanced at Annabel, almost as white as the patient, and nodded briefly. "I will wait downstairs."

He had found both Weem and Janet awaiting him. His batman had handed him a glass.

"A drop o' the right stuff, guv'nor. It'll put heart into you."

Hal had sniffed, and found it to be brandy. "I will not ask where you had this."

Weem had looked sly. "I've me ways, guv'nor. Aye, and acquaintance roundabouts."

"I don't doubt." He had tossed off the brandy, and had felt the better for it.

Janet had been looking excessively anxious, wringing her apron with restless fingers. "Shall I go up, Captain?"

"There isn't room enough, Janet. That's why I came down." He had dismissed her with a word of advice. "Why don't you begin upon your preparations for dinner. Whatever happens, we will still have to eat.''

He had nodded to Weem to follow, knowing that his presence was likely to afford Janet's mind a degree of distraction. He could only wish now that he had something to distract himself!

For years he had seen his comrades wounded, often in agony. He had watched men die, and seen in Spanish villages the rotting corpses of those butchered by marauding gangs—men, women and children. But nothing in his past had prepared him for the hideous dread that attacked him when the life of his own child was in question.

Say what he would to tell himself he had no reason to suppose Becky to be in such an extreme of danger, he could not rid himself of the fear. What price Annabel's mental state, then, if he could not control his own?

But Annabel had the advantage of him. She had nursed her daughter through a number of childhood illnesses. Nothing dreadfully serious, but bad enough for her to know the resilience of her little girl.

As she watched Dr Pettifer carry out a thorough examination, she was apprehensive but not yet swamped with dread. Almost immediately after Hal had left them, she had emerged from her first shock. And the instant Weem had arrived, with Rebecca carried in his arms, she had acted with authority and relative calm.

Within moments, Becky had been carefully changed from her wet clothes into her nightgown, and placed in Annabel's bed. She had directed Janet to put a brick on the stove in case it should be necessary to warm the child, though the day was hot. And by the time Hal returned with Dr Pettifer, she had a jug of lemonade by the bed in case of Becky waking in thirst, and she was regularly bathing her forehead with lavender water.

She reposed complete trust in Dr Pettifer. He was a tall man, rather thin, with a pinched look that, in Annabel's opinion, in no way expressed the reality of his character. He was one of the kindest men she knew, and he was master of his business. He had a gentle way with children that had endeared him to Becky, and he knew her history as well as Annabel did herself, for he had treated her from the first.

But when he put the covers back over the little form, he looked grave as he turned. With a finger to his lips, he moved to the door and beckoned Annabel out of the bedchamber. His voice dropped to a murmur.

"I am a trifle concerned, Mrs Lett."

Her heart lurched. "Oh, what is it?"

He eyed her in a manner that added considerably to her discomfort. "Let us go downstairs. She will not suffer for a moment or two alone."

Annabel followed him down, and at once saw Hal, standing stock still, his eyes trained upon the staircase. The instant she reached the bottom of the stairs, he came to her.

"How is she?"

She gripped his hand as he took her fingers within his own. "Dr Pettifer is just going to tell me. He says he is concerned, Hal!"

She turned to the doctor, who had taken up a stance by the table, setting his bag at his feet.

"Well?" demanded Hal, on a harsh note.

"I'm afraid there is little to be known just yet," said Dr Pettifer. "What troubles me is that the child may have suffered a concussion."

Annabel felt her stomach muscles clench. "What does that mean?"

It was Hal who answered. "A blow on the head sufficient to cause prolonged unconsciousness—and possible damage."

Annabel's eyes shot back to the doctor. "Is that true?"

He nodded. "In principle."

"What sort of damage?"

"It is useless to make any prognosis upon these matters until the patient wakes."

Annabel clutched Hal's hand, and braced herself, her voice steely. "Pray don't try to spare me. Tell me the worst, or I shall imagine it for myself and drive myself into a frenzy."

Pettifer looked at Hal, who shifted stiff shoulders.

"Tell her anything she wants to know. She has a right."

The doctor nodded, and became brisk. "It may affect Rebecca's sight, or her ability to think clearly. Or it may be nothing at all."

"What must I do for her?" asked Annabel tensely.

"Keep her warm. It is a hot day, but we must guard against fever. You had been using lavender water on her brow, and that is an excellent thing. And the moment she wakes, send for me again."

"May I give her a drink or food while we wait for you to arrive?"

"Water at first, then a little warm milk. Nothing more. Be sure I will be with you as speedily as I can come."

Annabel watched him pick up his bag and cross towards the front door. A species of panic made her pull her hand from Hal's and run after him.

''Doctor! How long will she be like this?''

''It may be a matter of hours. A word of warning, ma'am. It is possible that she may not recognise you—at first. Do not alarm yourself unduly. Be glad only that she wakes up!''

With which dread words, he executed a brief bow and left them. Annabel stood rooted to the spot, numb with horror as the implication sank into her brain. That Becky might be in some way impaired was one thing. That she could lose her altogether had not crossed her mind.

Hardly knowing what she did, Annabel turned slowly, and regarded Hal's face across the room. Incongruously, the likeness struck her, more than it had ever done since his arrival. Abruptly it came to her just why Rebecca was so very important. It was not merely that she loved her daughter for herself, but that Hal and she had made her—together.

Without a word, she stretched out her hand. Hal came to her, drawn less by the gesture than by the trouble in the vibrant green eyes. He took her into his arms, and pressed her head into his shoulder.

''It will be well, my darling. She will be well.''

Chapter Ten

Annabel was dog tired. She had lost all count of time. She knew she had slept for a while, for Hal had brought Janet to keep watch on Becky at some time in the night. Annabel's protests had gone unheeded, and he had marched her downstairs and made her lie on the truckle bed in his own room.

She had thought she would not sleep for worry, for the hours had come and gone and Becky had not wakened. But in no time at all, someone was shaking her shoulder and a grey light was creeping into the room as she opened her eyes.

"Go up now," came from the shadowed form that was Hal. "I have told Weem to wake me in three hours."

Which cryptic utterance had given her to understand that Hal had been up with their daughter for the better part of the night. Annabel was still fully dressed, except for her cap, and she dragged herself up from the bed.

"Is there no change?"

She caught the movement in the dimness as he shook his head. "But she is breathing easily. There seems to be no sign of fever, I am glad to say."

Annabel smiled her relief, and left him. Upstairs, she resumed her vigil, and her tears ran unchecked as she watched her little girl's still features, so small and white upon her own pillows. Had she come this far, suffered so much, only to be stricken down with this unbearable loss at the very point of snatching at the cup of happiness?

She took the minute hand into her fingers and kissed its smooth skin, still baby-soft and pudgy in its early growth. How far away, how unimportant now seemed that bank of pride that had been driving her! How foolish the ceaseless quarrels, and her stubborn holding to her bitter hurt. As foolish had she been as her father with his unrelenting vengeance.

But it was not too late. Hal's care of her now, and his devotion to his daughter—for hours he must have been in this very room, guarding Becky!—argued feelings that were balm in this hour of desperate need. And if she should prove to have misread him, there would be no more hesitation on her part. If she must humble herself to keep him, she would do it! Beg, if need be, as she now begged her Maker for deliverance of this precious bond whose joyful presence had been her own salvation.

As the dawn grew into day, however, she had little thought to spare for the strife-torn tangle of her relationship with Hal. Rebecca's condition appeared to worsen, for the stillness left her, and she began to fidget and whimper in her sleep.

"Hush, my love!" urged Annabel, seeking to quiet her with stroking motions of her hands. "Hush, my little one, Mama is here."

But the child's restless movements did not abate, and by the time Janet came in with a cup of tea for Annabel, her cheeks had become a trifle flushed and Annabel was alarmed.

"Janet, pray go and wake the Captain and ask him to send again to Dr Pettifer."

"He's already awake," Janet reported. "He was coming up when he'd had a wash, he said."

"Pray tell him to go immediately!" begged Annabel, impatient of this history.

She ushered the maid from the room, and almost lost her temper when Hal walked in a few minutes later.

"Why are you here?" she demanded, low-voiced. "I told Janet to—"

"I have sent Weem," he interrupted without ceremony, brushing past her to the bed. "What is amiss with her?"

"I do not know, but she has been restless and fidgety for a while, and you can see how flushed she is."

Hal bent over the child, setting a hand to her brow. "She is a little warm. God send it is not fever!"

Annabel looked at him piteously. "Do you think it is? You know more of these things than I."

"I am not a doctor, however." He took the cloth that was soaking in a bowl of lavender water and squeezed it out. "The day is excessively hot again," he observed as he laid the cloth to her forehead. "It may be that she is merely feeling the heat. It might help to remove the covers."

But Annabel would not countenance any such action until the doctor should approve it. She consented to open a window, however, and within a few minutes, as the clearer air circulated in the room, Rebecca did grow calmer.

Annabel sank down on the bed beside the pillows, Hal having taken up the place where she had previously been sitting. For several moments, neither of them spoke, for both had their eyes trained upon their daughter's features, and the bright hair spilling across the pillow.

"She is so beautiful," murmured Hal.

"She is very much your daughter."

His gaze came up. "I see her mother in her too."

Annabel shifted her shoulders, as if to shrug was too much movement in the needed quiet of the bedchamber. "That likeness escapes me. She has your eyes, though hers are bluer, perhaps. And your hair."

"And my temperament," he agreed with a smile. "But your obstinacy, Annabel. Which I know will bring her through this."

Annabel's eyes dropped to her daughter's face again. Suddenly excited, she put out a hand to seize Hal's arm.

"Her eyes are open!"

Hal's glance went down. Becky was staring up at him. His heart lurched. He could not tell from her expression what sort of condition she was in, but instinct made him shift off the bed, motioning to Annabel.

"You had better come here so that she can see you."

She slid round quickly, and gently picked up

Rebecca's hand, holding it with both her own. Her instant joy became tempered with apprehension as the child's eyes seemed rather to follow Hal than to focus upon herself.

"Becky?"

The small head turned on the pillow. For a few breathless instants, Annabel froze as her daughter gazed up into her face without reaction. Then her rosebud of a mouth opened.

"Mama?"

How the news had spread, Annabel did not know. But in the way of country villages, it had done so, and the messages of commiseration and goodwill began arriving even with the doctor's gig.

Dr Pettifer performed a number of tests—much against Rebecca's will—and pronounced her to be clear of any impairment.

"We appear to have had a miraculous escape, Mrs Lett. I can find nothing amiss."

The relief was intense. As a precautionary measure, however, the doctor required the child to rest quietly in bed another few days, and to Annabel's unenviable lot fell the task of keeping her there. Within two days, Rebecca was her usual bouncy self, and disinclined to remain between sheets.

That she did so remain for a further spell was

due to Hal's inspiration, for he suddenly bethought him of Kitty. To have the black kitten bounding about the bed, pouncing upon her toes, made Becky giggle with delight. And when Kitty slept, curled in a ball under her stroking hand, purring mightily, she was content herself to lie quiet and listen to a story.

After that, Hal took turns with Annabel at minding the child, leaving the two servants to deal with the household chores, with the result that there had been little opportunity for private converse. Meals were taken apart, each eating at need of whatever had been prepared.

It seemed to Hal that they were only together briefly when there was company downstairs. Common civility demanded that those who took the trouble to visit to enquire after Becky's health should at least be thanked in person.

By the end of the week, however, Dr Pettifer pronounced Rebecca to be well enough to be permitted to resume all her former pursuits. Which was as well, for the child was increasingly difficult to manage, and not even Hal—to whose peremptory demands she had once or twice been brought to attend—could prevent her from racing about the cottage or the garden. September had dawned, but the weather had continued fine, if not as hot, and the doctor had allowed that Rebecca might be brought outside.

The relaxation of her regime proved a signal for the resumption of normal life, and it was only then that Hal realised that nothing had been settled between himself and Annabel since the interruption of that last passionate encounter.

It was only when Mr Maperton called that the matter was recalled to his mind at all. It was on Monday the seventh, a few days past the lawyer's appointed time. He had not wished, he said, to disturb the preoccupied parents with business at a distressing moment. Maperton's errand was to ask whether the Captain wished to retain the Empty House. It was then borne in upon Hal that he did not know! Nothing had been discussed, nothing had been decided. He had no notion whether they would stay or go. There was nothing for it but to take the Empty House for a further month.

When he had informed Annabel, she had looked at him blankly, as if she had not understood.

"The Empty House?"

"With this crisis, I thought it would be best to defer any decisions."

Hal thought an odd look passed over her face, but she had agreed readily enough—if with a somewhat strange response.

"I cannot think about it now."

He dropped the subject, feeling distanced by her evident preoccupation. But since Becky had returned to sleeping in her own room, the vacant place beside Annabel was preying upon Hal's mind. Yet she apparently had her attention still upon the little girl. He was loath to appear precipitate. He did not wish Annabel to suppose he had been waiting only for their daughter to remove from her bed in order to install himself there in her stead. With what patience he could muster, he bided his time.

Annabel hid in the vegetable garden, retching horribly. Her hand trembled where it held on to a convenient branch of the cherry tree. There had been too many mornings now when she had been obliged to sneak away. At first she had thought— hoped!—it was merely the aftermath of exhaustion from Rebecca's illness. When it had persisted, she wondered if perhaps she had eaten something that did not agree with her.

Wondered? Oh, dissembler that she was! She had known—how could she not?—in the first instance. Her wonderings were merely the desperate attempt to pretend to herself that this was not happening. It was why she had steadfastly rejected the idea of applying to Dr Pettifer on her own account. She dreaded to hear what he must inevitably tell her. As if she did not already know it!

What was there in the power of Hal's seed? Or was it her own unlucky lot to be ever fertile? Oh, that this should not have come upon her now! The last thing she had wanted was to appeal again to Hal's sense of honour and duty. If it was selfish, then so be it. She did not want him to stay for the unknown being that she was certain must be growing in her womb. She wanted him to stay because he wanted to stay with her. Because he loved her.

If only Rebecca's unfortunate accident had not interrupted them that day! He had been within an ace of giving her that assurance she so badly needed. Had he not kissed her with a violent intensity, and dared her to say that it was duty? And during the horrid time while their daughter lay at danger, all his actions might have been chosen to prove a fond devotion.

Yet he had not said anything! He had made no amorous move towards her since Rebecca's emergence from the sick-room. And he had made no attempt to renew that interrupted discussion.

Annabel knew that she was equally guilty. Had she not promised herself, while Rebecca lay deathly quiet in her bed, that she would throw aside all pride and beg him to remain? Only she had not known then with what a further complication she had to contend.

The nausea had passed, and sighing, Annabel washed away the residue with the perfumed water with which she'd had the forethought to provide herself. She carried it back towards the kitchen, walking with slow steps while the nagging questions continued to turn around her mind.

She avoided Janet's suspicious eye as she laid the jug down. In vain.

"What's to do? You're looking downright peaky, ma'am."

"I am perfectly well," lied Annabel. "It is merely hot outside."

The maid glanced through the window at the lowering sky. The unusually fine weather for the time of year had at last given way to a stiff breeze and ominous clouds.

"Tell that to the Captain when he asks you!" advised Janet brusquely.

Annabel eyed her in some alarm. "Does he know I was out?"

Janet sniffed, lifting a lid to stir a pot on the stove. "Gone up to the Empty House in a dudgeon."

A stir of apprehension troubled Annabel's breast. "How do you know he was in a dudgeon?"

"Damned Weem, damned the Marquis, and stomped off, only because Weem was talking of the murder," announced Janet comprehensively.

"Who is with Rebecca?"

"No need to be anxious, ma'am. Weem is showing her card tricks. She's happy as a grig."

Going through into the family room, Annabel discovered her daughter sitting entranced at the table, with Kitty curled up in her lap, and the batman engaged in a sleight of hand series of magic and conjuring effects for her delectation.

Satisfied, Annabel left them and went upstairs to her bedchamber to check that her recent sickness had not disarranged her hair. She had taken to leaving off her cap, in a half-conscious attempt to render herself more attractive, for her hair was one of her few attributes that she knew Hal appreciated. She had caught him glancing at her now and then, and longed for him to speak.

Her black locks had indeed become disarranged. Annabel removed the pins and let them loose, seizing up the brush and plying it vigorously. Her hair had grown, falling about her shoulders in heavy folds. Loose, it dropped forward, thinning her cheeks.

Pausing, Annabel stared at her image in the mirror. Of what use to pine? This was what she was, and Hal had ever found her to his taste—no matter her own opinion of her lack of beauty. Had she not proof within her of the violence of his passion? What more did she want? If he did not love her in the way she wanted to be loved, was it not better to have what he could willingly give her, than to live without him?

The thought of which caused a wrench at her heart. No. She could not endure it. Better to have him on any terms, than not to have him at all! If he chose to stay because she was the mother of his children, she would accept it. Let her not add to her father's malevolence and destroy her own life. Hal was here, with her, with his daughter. And that was by his choice. Why should she have the arrogance to demand more?

For what had she to wait? It was near two months since his arrival, was it not? What day was it? Thursday. Then it was the tenth. Hal had come here on the eleventh of July. There was no sense in dragging this out any longer.

She must tell him. And she must do it now, before her resolution had a chance to fail. In haste, she did no more than pull her hair back, pinning it either side merely to keep it off her face. Then she got up, snatched a shawl from a peg upon the door, and rapidly left the cottage.

Staring from the front window of the Empty House, Hal caught sight of Annabel as she came out of the trees and crossed on to the overgrown approach that led to the house.

He found himself riveted. She was walking with a brisk determination that spoke of urgency, clutching a flowered shawl about the shoulders of her muslin gown. Had something happened? Instinct encouraged him to go to meet her, but he found himself mesmerised by the swing of the loose fall of raven tresses.

She looked up, and halted, staring at the window. She must have seen him. He could not make out the green eyes, but there was that in her look which threw him into momentary panic. She was seeking him out for a purpose. God send she had not once more set her mind against him!

Then Annabel began to move again, her steps slow. Hal wrenched himself away from the window and went with quick strides through into the square hall. He opened the front door, and held it wide.

Annabel was but a few feet away, and she checked again. Hal's features were set in stern lines. Oh, if her courage did not fail! Had she chosen her moment badly?

His tone was terse. "What is it?"

He saw her mouth quiver. The devil! He had not meant to sound unwelcoming. He stood aside and gestured her into the house.

"You will take cold if you stand there."

Annabel's apprehension eased a trifle at the warmer note. She walked past him into the hall, her gaze lowered.

Hal led the way into the large front room. "I was thinking that this would be the most comfortable substitute for your large room at End Cottage. One would be tempted to use it for a parlour, but I think you might find that a waste."

She might find it so? Annabel crossed to the front window so that he might not see the horrid fear that gripped her. Did he mean her to take this place, after all? Was he again thinking of leaving?

Crossing aimlessly to the other window to one side, which led on to an expansive garden, Hal's mind was far removed from what he had said. He had merely thrown it out for want of any other way to explain his being discovered staring from the window, when he had allegedly come up here to work.

Annabel fought down her doubts, and turned. "Janet said you had left the cottage in a dudgeon."

He looked round. "Is that why you came?"

She knew not how to reply. She had come for something quite other, but now that she was face to face with Hal, she had no notion how to begin. But prevarication would only drag out the difficulty. She drew a breath, and met his gaze full.

"No. I wanted to talk to you."

Hal could not help himself. "It is about time!"

Annabel winced. "I had not meant to leave it so long."

He threw out a hand. "I am as much to blame, Annabel. I beg your pardon."

She eyed him. "You left in haste, and in displeasure. And your temper is on a short rein. Are you angry with me?"

"With myself rather. I have allowed things to ride when I should instead have forced a conclusion." Hal gave a mirthless laugh. "And then that rascal Weem must prose on and on about Sywell's murderer, in whose identity I must confess to have scant interest."

But Annabel had no ears for this divagation. What conclusion? He must mean the situation between them! She was conscious of a flurry at her heart. Had he reached a decision? Did he mean after all to adhere to that resolve which, she would swear, he had been about to renounce on the day of Rebecca's accident?

"What did you want to talk to me about?"

Annabel jumped. He was watching her, a grave look in his face. She tried to speak, to open the discussion, but could not. Lamely, she prevaricated.

"About—about us. Our situation."

"Yes," he responded heavily. "We should certainly discuss that. I confess I have been holding back from it."

She managed to smile. "And I. We have had a great deal else to think of."

"Not for several days, however."

Now was the moment for Annabel to announce that she had indeed had her mind on another matter these last days. And then she must add that it was something which would remove all choice from his path. Once he knew of it, she had not the slightest doubt that nothing in the world would induce him to leave—no matter her feelings.

The knowledge stilled her tongue. How had she supposed she could say it? How make him suffer all over again the remorse and guilt that had spilled from the pages of his letters? And at last the dread truth hit her.

Why had she not thought of it before? Or perhaps she had. Dormant in the far reaches of her mind, she must have known. It must account for her reluctance to come to this moment of revelation. In her conscious mind at last, it was so obvious that she wondered at her own stupidity.

How was she ever to convince Hal that she loved him, when she was for the second time at the mercy of her need? The sheer impossibility of it threw her into sudden anguish. She put her hands to her face, dislodging the shawl which slipped off her shoulders to the floor. Her voice cracked.

"What am I to do? *What am I to do?*"

Hal had watched, with growing consternation, the build of trouble in her face. That she had come to him with a matter of import became increasingly clear, and dismay began to hollow at his chest. But at this outburst, he started forward without thought or hesitation.

"What is it, Annabel?" he demanded urgently, grasping her hands as they dropped from her face. "What is the matter? Tell me!"

"I cannot!" she cried, trying to pull her hands away. "I thought I could. I knew I must. But it is altogether too distressing!"

Hal dropped her hands and grasped her shoulders. "Annabel, calm yourself! Come, there is no need for this. Have we not passed the stage of being reticent with one another? I know I have held off these many days—"

"And I!" she uttered wildly. "I have never been so afraid that I will lose you again. Oh, not in the flesh, for I know you will not leave when once you hear—"

She broke off abruptly, realising how she had almost betrayed her new condition. But Hal was frowning now, a look of puzzlement in his face. His grip relaxed, but he held her between his hands.

"Lose me? Annabel, after what we have been through with Rebecca, there is nothing on God's earth that would induce me to leave you!"

A little of the jumping panic in her abated. She stared blankly. "Are you serious?"

Hal released her, letting out a shaky laugh. "I have never been more so. Devil take it, how do you think I could live away from you? Either of you! I would spend my days in a ceaseless worry that some harm threatened you both, and I not there to do my damndest against it."

Annabel's pulse began a slow tattoo. "Then you do care!"

"Good God, have I not made it abundantly clear?"

"But you spoke just now of hesitation! I thought you meant to imply that you wished again to discuss the matter of your departure."

"After what has passed between us?" He threw up a hand and ran it through his hair in a gesture of frustration. "I tell you, Annabel, even had you not softened towards me, I should have endured living with your hatred rather than take one step out of your life!"

The tattoo pulsed into a crescendo, deafening in her own ears. Yet a protest rose to her lips. "But you have not said so! You never told me, Hal."

He uttered an amazed laugh. "You can say that? You, who could not bring yourself to admit that you wanted me to stay. Yet it was in your eyes, in your movements, in every gesture. Oh, but you are stubborn, Annabel!"

Her eyes filled. "No longer." She came to him, holding out her hands. "Let me be first to say it, because I am most to be disbelieved."

He took her hands and drew her to him, tenderness in his tone. "I will not disbelieve the evidence of my own eyes."

Annabel released one of her hands, and her fingers came up, trembling at his cheek. "Then know that I love you—still. For I never stopped loving you. I tried, God knows! But in vain. Hal, I am so thankful that you came back to me!''

Hal's own hand was trembling as he stroked the black hair away from her face and held it so. ''I wonder if you have any notion what that means to me. The only difference, my darling, is that I never tried to stop.''

''Oh, Hal!''

He drew her into his arms. ''I have loved you from the first, and from the first I have known that I could never cease to love you.''

Then his lips found hers, in a kiss of the utmost gentleness. He pulled away, and Annabel melted at the unprecedented warmth in his eyes. For a moment or two he regarded her without speaking, as if he must drink in the sight.

Then he was kissing her again, with all the fire and passion that had ever exploded between them. But Annabel felt a new quality in it. One of—yes, possession! She thrilled to the feeling, and knew that her surrender would be a thousand times her gain.

At length Hal released her mouth, and raised his head to look at her. The softened look in her face warmed his heart. But a snatch of memory came back to him, and he frowned as he cradled her face.

"Why did you suppose that I should disbelieve you?"

Annabel suffered an instant qualm. He must have seen it, for he released her a little and his frown deepened.

"You look dismayed." Abruptly he remembered the frantic words with which she had thrown open the way for these confessions of love. "There is something distressing you! Surely you cannot be afraid to tell me, Annabel."

Her lip quivered. "I should not be, I know. Perhaps I am yet unused to have faith."

Hal caught her fingers in his. "If so, it is not your fault. Circumstance has moulded you. But if there is aught I should know—"

A horrid notion assailed him. The question was out of his mouth before he could stop it.

"Do you mean to tell me that in these years we were apart, you have known another man?"

For an instant, Annabel felt herself tense up with all the furious resentment that she had shown him when he came. She hit back without thought.

"If I had, do you suppose I would have given myself to you again like a common whore?"

Hal was already regretting the random thought. He caught her to him. "Forgive me! I never meant to say such a thing to you." Then he drew away so that he might look into her face. "Only I am so fiercely jealous of you, Annabel! You don't know how much. When Weem brought me the news that you were married, before I could recall that Lett had been your mother's maiden name, I was positively murderous towards that phantom Captain who had allegedly taken you to wife."

But Annabel's anger had disappeared as swiftly as it came. How could she protest against an attitude that only provided her with further proof of his feelings. Instead it gave her courage—impatience even!—to say what she must.

"Never mind that now, Hal. I was afraid that once you heard I was again with child, you would think that any love I might express was unreal. You would believe—"

Hal broke in without ceremony. "What did you say?"

Abruptly realising that she had already said it, Annabel broke into laughter. "Oh, Hal, and my tongue would not utter the words when I wanted it to!"

Dazedly, he tried to take it in. "Again? We have done it again?"

A little shy, Annabel nodded, reaching up to smooth his moustache in an affectionate gesture.

"I don't know how it is, but it seems you have barely to touch me, and I must fall."

"Are you sure?"

"As sure as I can be, for the sickness that has affected me these many days. It was just the same with Rebecca, but it passed after a few weeks."

Slowly it began to penetrate. And with it came a glow at Hal's chest which threatened to burst with the swelling there.

Annabel saw his eyes rim with wetness, and knew that her anxiety had been needless. She reached her face to his and softly kissed him. He returned the kiss strongly, but in a moment she found herself held by the arms. Determination was in every line of his face, and in his voice.

"This time you will marry me! I am not content to remain as Captain Lett, and you will not again give birth to an illegitimate child."

Annabel could not but be moved by his vehemence. And the thought that this pregnancy would be attended by the care and comfort of a husband at her side—in stark contrast to the horrid secrecy and despair of the first—was unutterably desirable. Yet there were shoals ahead, and she sighed.

"I am very willing, Hal, but how are we to do? Nothing could please me more than to leave here, but—"

''Yes, let us leave Steep Ride. I have my estate. We will marry and live there as Captain and Mrs Colton. No one in the area—aside from my brother Ned and his wife—will know any different.''

It was a programme infinitely attractive to her, but she could not let it pass unchallenged. ''That is all very well, Hal, but unless we are to live entirely retired, it is sure to come out. We cannot forever avoid acquaintance with everyone who might possibly know of my life here in Steep Ride. I am bound to be recognised sooner or later.''

''We will deal with that as it arises,'' Hal said firmly. He released her and went to pick up her shawl. ''Besides, I have no intention to making a figure in society. It is just as likely that we will meet no one from one year's end to the other who has the least acquaintance with you.''

''To be truthful, there are few persons here that I would wish to see again! Apart from Jane. And Charlotte has gone now. Indeed, of all those I have met, I would most regret Serena, especially as she is in the same condition as myself.''

She felt him place the shawl about her shoulders again, but her attention had caught. Serena had met her here, but this was not her home. And Serena, as Lady Wyndham, had become a personage of great influence.

"Oh, I know what to do!"

"As long as it does not preclude our marriage—"

"Do be quiet, Hal, and listen! I will throw myself upon the mercy of Serena, and—"

"Who in Hades is Serena?"

"You met her! Oh, it was in that first week, so I dare say you do not remember. Lady Wyndham—she came to visit me."

Hal frowned in an effort of memory. "A youthful creature? Extremely lovely with golden hair?"

"She is extraordinarily beautiful, yes. I might have known you would notice that, you wretch!"

He grinned, and quickly leaned to kiss her. "I had the greatest difficulty in calling her to mind, so you may be satisfied. But how such a young female can be of use to you, I do not pretend to guess."

Annabel told him a little of Serena's unheralded arrival at her cottage that far-off day in the previous year, which had led to her coming especially to visit on her return home.

"She was insistent that she would stand my friend. I will tell her the truth, and I do not think she will judge me harshly. But she is going to be a countess, Hal, so her patronage must protect me."

"You mean if she visits you, then others will not dare to speak against you? Yes, that is the way of the world."

"It may be despicable," said Annabel with a grimace, "but there is no denying it is useful. My respectability has been hardly won, Hal, and I should not care to lose it."

He drew her into his arms. "You must do as you see fit, my darling, but for my part, I care nothing for what anyone may say. As long as I may at last call you in truth my beloved wife, that is all that matters to me."

The last vestiges of doubt were swept away. Annabel gave her lips up to his, in the sure knowledge that the passion that consumed them both had its origin in a deep and abiding affinity that could never be destroyed. And if there were duty and honour involved, why that, in the man she loved, was all to the good.

* * * * *

HARLEQUIN®
Makes any time special ®

AMERICAN *Romance*

Upbeat, All-American Romances

Duets™

Romantic Comedy

Harlequin® Historical

Historical, Romantic Adventure

HARLEQUIN®
INTRIGUE

Romantic Suspense

Harlequin Romance®

Capturing the World You Dream O

HARLEQUIN® *Presents*

Seduction and passion guaranteed

HARLEQUIN® *Super* ROMANCE®

Emotional, Exciting, Unexpected

HARLEQUIN® *Temptation*

Sassy, Sexy, Seductive!

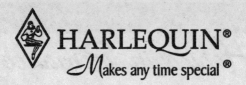

HARLEQUIN®
Makes any time special ®

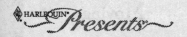
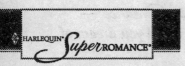

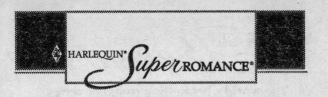

HARLEQUIN Presents

The world's bestselling romance series...
The series that brings you your favorite authors,
month after month:

Helen Bianchin...Emma Darcy
Lynne Graham...Penny Jordan
Miranda Lee...Sandra Marton
Anne Mather...Carole Mortimer
Susan Napier...Michelle Reid

and many more uniquely talented authors!

Wealthy, powerful, gorgeous men...
Women who have feelings just like your own...
The stories you love, set in exotic, glamorous locations...

HARLEQUIN Presents

Seduction and passion guaranteed!

HARLEQUIN®
INTRIGUE

WE'LL LEAVE YOU BREATHLESS!

If you've been looking for thrilling tales of
contemporary passion and sensuous love stories
with taut, edge-of-the-seat suspense—then
you'll love Harlequin Intrigue!

Every month, you'll meet four new heroes
who are guaranteed to make your spine tingle
and your pulse pound. With them you'll enter
into the exciting world of Harlequin Intrigue—
where your life is on the line
and so is your heart!

THAT'S INTRIGUE—
ROMANTIC SUSPENSE
AT ITS BEST!

HARLEQUIN®
Makes any time special ®

Harlequin® Historical

From rugged lawmen and valiant knights to defiant heiresses and spirited frontierswomen, Harlequin Historicals will capture your imagination with their dramatic scope, passion and adventure.

Harlequin Historicals... they're too good to miss!

HHDIR1